That Ghoul Ava
Sacks the Quarterback!

(The boyfriend episode.)

TW Brown

authortwbrown.com

Estacada, Oregon, USA

ISBN 978-1-940734-56-9

Other Titles by TW Brown

The DEAD Series:

DEAD: The Ugly Beginning
DEAD: Revelations
DEAD: Fortunes & Failures
DEAD: Winter
DEAD: Siege & Survival
DEAD: Confrontation
DEAD: Reborn
DEAD: Darkness Before Dawn
DEAD: Spring
DEAD: Reclamation
DEAD: Blood & Betrayal
DEAD: End

DEAD Special Edition

DEAD: Perspectives Story (Vols. 1 & 2)
DEAD: Vignettes (Vols. 1 & 2)
DEAD: The Geeks (Vols. 1 & 2)

DEAD: Snapshot— {Insert Town Here}

*DEAD: Snapshot—**Portland, Oregon***
*DEAD: Snapshot—**Leeds, England*** (August 2015)

Zomblog

Zomblog
Zomblog II
Zomblog: The Final Entry
Zomblog: Snoe
Zomblog: Snoe's War
Zomblog: Snoe's Journey

That Ghoul Ava

That Ghoul Ava: Her First Adventures
That Ghoul Ava & The Queen of the Zombies
That Ghoul Ava Kick Some Faerie A**
Next, on a very special That Ghoul Ava
That Ghoul Ava…on the Lam!
That Ghoul Ava On a Roll

You can find my titles
on Audio as well.

Audible.com

For Pamela

Thank you for giving Ava your voice

A moment with the author…

I love Ava Birch. What started as a "Thank You" gift to one of my very first fans has grown into something special that I enjoy returning to in between all the zombies and rock stars. As she develops, a story has finally unfolded that hopefully will take several adventures to tell.

To be honest, there was a time when the release of an Ava story was met with a certain bittersweetness. It simply did not release to the types of sales that a new *DEAD* would see. It still has a long way to go before it reaches those sorts of numbers, but I can say that they are increasing with each subsequent volume.

No writer likes to see something they labor lovingly over become generally ignored. I'd be lying if I made any other claim than the one where I say I would love to sell more of the *That Ghoul Ava* adventures…and maybe one day that will be the case. However, despite the numbers I will continue to write these stories because I love them. I am just honest when I say that I am glad more of you seem to be doing the same. Now…if I could just figure out a way to get some reader reviews on Amazon (and Audible).

Big thanks to all the people who keep things fun. Caroline Harmon for being the first official (and unofficial) president of the *That Ghoul Ava* fan club; Elizabeth, Nancy, Randy and Terri for being part of the Ava Beta Team (fun to say…just try it!). And I really do want to thank you for coming along on the adventure. Without you, I'd just be one hand clapping.

"Look at all the people here tonight!"
TW Brown
January 2016

Contents

1

Little Lies

"You moon-faced idiot!" I screamed at the top of my lungs. Every bit of fury I possessed was focused on that one solitary black and white striped monster that seemed both oblivious to my scorn as well as unconcerned.

I glanced over at Race and saw the agitation etched in his face as well. While I might be considerably more vocal with my displeasure, I rested in the comfort that Race Mitchell was on my side of this little outburst.

A cascade of noise showered down on the monster as he took ten very deliberate steps. Without a care in the world, he placed the prolate-spheroid on the green surface and then turned to face my direction.

"Holding, number fifty-seven on the offense. That is a ten-yard penalty from the spot of the foul...and fourth down." He blew his whistle and wound his arms in a circle to signal the start of the clock.

I turned to Race, making every effort to keep my switch-digits as well as Sharkmouth from making an unwelcome appearance. "But we had the winning touchdown!" I pleaded, my voice dangerously close to that whining pitch that I hate in myself almost as much as I loathe hearing it in others. "How is it that every time we have done something positive on this drive, that stupid ref comes up with some mystical sort of call?"

"Haters gotta hate," he said with uncharacteristic venom.

I don't know which had me more taken aback. The tone of malice in his voice, or the fact that he had pulled out a pithy and common phrase like that and used it so deftly. It was sorta like sitting next to the president and hearing him let one rip.

My eyes shot up to the scoreboard. I could not choose where to maintain my focus as my glance bounced back and forth between the players scrambling on the field to get to the line of scrimmage and get the play off before the numbers reached zero; or the clock itself which marched on unerringly downwards.

5...

4...

3...

2...

"Hut!" I heard a voice above all the others bark.

The ball was in the quarterback's hands and he was dropping back. I saw our Treyvon Webb shooting down the far side of the field. He was making no pretense of even glancing back as he zoomed towards the end zone. On the side nearest me, Tony Percy was doing the same thing. Both of the players had two members of the opposing team right on their heels.

I found the quarterback again as he ducked under the outstretched arms of a man that easily had a hundred pounds on him, and thus, lacked both the speed and the dexterity to catch the elusive Colt Faber. The agile man stopped on a dime as a second defensive player lunged at him. He sprung straight back and was running laterally almost faster than my eyes could track...and that is saying something since I am a ghoul with more than a few enhanced powers at my disposal.

The clock had hit double zeroes and that meant that this game was all over after this play. I felt something jostle me and I tore my eyes from the clock to see Faber being dragged down from behind...but not before he heaved that football with all his might.

When had I stood up? I wondered as my eyes tracked the ball in flight as it arced up, reached its apex, and then began its missile-like decent. It was coming down towards the hands of Treyvon Webb and a member of the visiting team.

There was a single moment just before the ball reached the end of its journey where time seemed to freeze. In that instant, only two outcomes were possible. If Webb catches the ball, our little upstart indoor football team remains undefeated and enters the playoffs with home field advantage throughout the playoffs...or he misses it and the zero under the loss column changes. That would put an official end to the "Quest for Perfection" which had become our team's rallying cry three weeks ago when one of our players—the stupid kicker of all people—had made the statement on camera that there was not a team remaining on the schedule that had the chance of knocking us off.

Obviously the kicker had not looked at that schedule and seen the hated squad from Arizona as the final home game before we entered the playoffs. Did I mention they were three-time repeating champions of the league?

There was a split second of silence as the ball vanished in between Webb and the defender. Then...Webb leapt into the air and thrust the ball skyward just as the official raised his hands to signal the touchdown. My eyes did a quick scan of the field. No signs of any more of those pesky little yellow flags.

"We did it!" I spun to Race and grabbed him in a hug. I felt my feet leave the ground for a second as he squeezed me tight and pulled me off the floor.

The crowd was going wild and blue, red, and silver confetti rained down on the field, showering our team as they all gathered together with their hands raised in victory. The team from Arizona was trudging away, heads down for the most part. A few stopped to shake hands with some of our boys, but most of them just vanished into the tunnel that took them to their locker room.

Eventually, the euphoria receded and the team began to depart—many having to climb back over the barricade after coming out to join the fans in the celebration. Race and I turned and started to file out into the night with all the other fans. Shouts echoed throughout the arena as people chanted the team's name or just let out whoops and hollers in exclamation of a great victory.

"I really did not think you would get into this," Race snickered as we exited the double doors and joined the throng of people searching for their cars.

"Me either," I replied with a laugh.

Seriously, I was really dubious when he said that he had season tickets to the local indoor football team's games and asked if I would like to join him for a game or two. After the first one, I told him I was in for the duration. It might have had something to do with the fact that we were down in the fourth row and on the second play of the game, one of our players crashed into the opponent and sent him flying over the wall.

I should probably give you a few more details. You see, in the front row were these two bimbos wearing way too much makeup and way too little clothing for a night out at a sporting event. Basically they looked like hookers. Anyway, they were also visibly intoxicated and making total fools of themselves by calling out to every player that passed by with various offers that only furthered their similarity to a street walker.

Both women had the largest and most over-priced of the stadium beers in their hands. When the collision happened and the opposing player got checked into the wall, I could tell that the momentum was going to take him over. When his feet slammed into the two large beers and sent up a miniature tidal wave of amber liquid…I started laughing.

Watching it play in slow motion on the massive screen hanging over the field only made me laugh harder. I seriously doubt that a single drop of that beer made it to the floor. Both of those women got it square in the face…and hair. I would guess that they had probably spent a few hours each getting their hair to look that perfect. And in just a matter of seconds, they both had what resembled a stringy, bleached blonde mop hanging down in their faces. Also, I don't think they sprung for the waterproof mascara either.

I laughed so hard that the human version of me would have probably wet her pants. One of them spun around and shot me what I am sure she believed was her nastiest glare. I laughed harder. Also, I might have let my dark glasses slip down just a bit to reveal my jet black orbs.

I never did see those two again. No worries, though. By the end of that first game, I was actually hooked on the sporting aspect of the event.

We stopped at the big black van and Race opened my door for me, gave me a hand as I climbed up and in, and then shut the door and came around the front to his side. I guess I wasn't really paying attention to anything specific…that is probably why that gigantic man ended up right beside my window without me realizing that he was there until he knocked on the glass.

Whether it was due to all the effort I'd used keeping my special talents like my switch-digit finger and toenails and Sharkmouth in check, or just the simple act of being spooked, I went what Race refers to as "full-ghoul" mode in a second.

Spinning on the person, I heard my own little sound of surprise matched by a yelp. Race had just opened his door, but in a flash he had a blade in his hand so quick that I had no time to actually wonder where it'd come from.

"Are you Ava Birch?" the man asked, foolishly ignoring the angry Templar that was skirting back around the front of the van.

I took a moment to really get a look at this guy. He was pretty big. I'm not talking giant-like, but for a human…big. His skin was a creamy sort of brown and I saw black dreadlocks hanging around and past his shoulders under the big coat he was wearing. I guessed him to be at least six and a half feet tall and nearing the three-hundred-pound mark…but he was not fat. His eyes were a chocolate brown and looked a little bloodshot. I didn't need my super sniffer to tell that he was a little bit tipsy.

"What the hell?" I whispered.

I had just realized that the normal smell of dying that all mortal humans give off was lacking here. This guy smelled like…rocks? Hmm…no, rocks don't really have a smell, do they.

"Half-troll," the man said as he reached out and caught

Race's arm as the Templar tried to grab him by one massive bicep. "My moms snagged my pops when he was out on a hunting trip with his buddies. She gave me over to him when I was just a little guy to be raised among the humans."

"I have a hard time believing that you were ever little," I said as I rolled my window down.

My eyes caught a flash of blue under the big overcoat and it struck me where I recognized the man from. "You're Anthony Riddle...the starting defensive lineman!" I tried not to gush, but seriously...this guy sacked more quarterbacks than any other two linemen this year put together and had set the league record around the halfway mark in the season. "I love watching you beat up offensive linemen who foolishly try to stop you."

"Yeah..." his voice sounded funny when he replied, and I could see his eyes darting around with what I could only guess to be nervousness. "Look, I have a problem, and the word is that you might be able to help."

I was puzzled. How on earth could I help this guy? My knowledge of football was at a pretty basic level.

"If I can help...I will," I finally said.

"Then meet me tomorrow night at—" Anthony started, but Race cut him off.

"If you are meeting with Ava, then you will do so at a place of her choosing...not yours." My big strong Templar was scowling. He was still rubbing his arm where the half-troll had grabbed him and moved him aside like a child. He quit as soon as he saw me looking. Men can be such morons.

I reached in my purse and pulled out a card. They had been Lisa's idea of a joke, but the joke was on her. Ever since the word had gotten out in the Supernatural community about how I'd dealt with those Valkyries, I'd become quite popular.

Morgan had commented on a few occasions that it might not be such a good thing; but I think she is just jealous. Plus, now that I am getting all these jobs, I am not as reliant on her for the scraps and such that she throws my way whenever she encounters something that she feels is beneath her.

Okay, maybe I am being a bit petty...but I think I've earned that right. I've saved her butt more than once, and actually, this new semi-celebrity status is practically her fault. She is the one who set me up for that job in Dallas with that roller derby team. Well…her and that fanged nuisance Belinda.

He is part troll, Ava, Blodwen's voice piped up from inside my head. *Be careful.*

The old gwyll had a point. None of my experiences with trolls up to now had gone very well. I'd been swallowed whole by a lake troll and don't get me started on that nasty little mud troll in the basement of the former Dallas Psychic's house.

Of all the current residents that lived inside my head, Blodwen was the only one that I pretty much gave free reign. She was like having a living Supernatural encyclopedia connected to my brain. Of course, she was also the one who kept the unruliest denizen of my mind under control.

Boudicca.

To those who may not know about this little gem of history, she apparently gave Roman emperor Nero fits. That is the short version. Oh…and she is also apparently the first female ghoul…at least that anybody knows about. Her current address is some deep, dark box in a corner of my mind.

(Hopefully this will be the only Ferris Bueller moment in this book: I could recap all the stuff that has led to this point, but seriously…who starts a book on the seventh volume? If you grabbed this book on a lark, either return it or go back to the beginning…this story will still be here when you catch up.)

"We can meet, but you need to tell me how a troll is pulling off being human and playing professional sports. Don't they have blood tests or something?" I asked, shooting a look over at Race that I hope conveyed the fact that I am a big ghoul and can take care of myself. Opening my doors is fine, but I handle my own fights, thank you very much.

"I am part human, and that means my blood is just like any other human. The differences would either not show up or not be anything that the doctors would be able to detect."

"Okay. So how about you come out to my place and we can meet." Yeah, it wasn't a question. I didn't fear this guy, but I am not stupid.

"Can I bring a friend?" Anthony asked, and he got a sheepish look on his face. "She's kind of a fan."

I heard Race do a terrible job of holding back a snort. I chose not to dignify his reaction with so much as a glance. And he could make all the noises he wanted, I was becoming known around our little community. After all, The Queen of the Zombies, a few giants, a couple of Psychics, a Valkyrie warrior, a powerful creature that is a member of the faerie line, and yes…a gigantic lake troll and a squishy mud troll have all fallen to me. Those are just the highlights.

"Sure, bring whoever you like." I nodded to the card he held in his hand. "The phone number will put you in touch with one of my people that will give you directions."

He nodded and turned around to walk away. I saw Race glare at the man's back until he vanished through a door back into the arena. Apparently satisfied, he came around and climbed into the driver's seat.

We were on the freeway headed home and driving in some pretty uncomfortable silence that I felt the need to break. "We're going to the playoffs!" I squealed.

"Maybe now this city will pay attention," Race grumbled.

That had been an issue for him all year. Apparently the local sports media did not take indoor football seriously. There was little to no coverage. I wasn't entirely sure what the big deal was, but it sure bugged the heck out of him. He always muttered something about how Portland was a sports-ignorant city that cared for nothing except basketball and soccer. I didn't have the heart to remind him that both basketball and soccer were sports.

"So, is the rumor true?" Race asked as we turned down the long, dark road that would eventually lead to my new house…or fortress to be more accurate.

"Depends on the rumor," I replied. I didn't need light to see perfectly, but glancing over, I could not help but get butterflies. His chiseled jaw and rugged face was even sexier in the green glow of the dashboard lights.

"I hear that Betty has returned."

8

I did everything in my power not to show any expression. I know that Race and I are just starting to head into that whole dating thing, but he is still a Templar. I am still a ghoul. His order was sworn to wipe all female ghouls out a long time ago. Our degree of trust has to contain different boundaries than say…Brad and Angelina.

"I don't know where you heard that, but if she is back…that is news to me."

Despite the potentially romantic relationship building between the two of us, there were certain things I was not yet ready to divulge to Race. I mean, we hadn't even 'sealed the deal' so to speak.

"Is that how you want to play this?" he muttered.

And it didn't look like tonight was going to be the night either. Another peek over at him and I could see the clench in his jaw…plus his chin was sticking out just a bit more than normal. He was taking on his role of hard-ass Templar.

Great.

"I'm not playing anything," I harrumphed. Okay, I am totally lying my butt off, but now that I've made my bed…

"Jesus, Ava, when are you gonna figure it out that I'm on your side?"

"When you stop interrogating me."

"Interrogating?" he shot back sarcastically. "I can assure you that there is never a doubt when I am interrogating somebody. I simply asked you a question."

"Find out who is making those little ray guns yet?" I turned to face him, crossing my arms over my chest.

I am pretty sure that I felt the van swerve just a teensy bit. I already knew the answer to that question, so yeah…I'm setting him up. Turnabout is fair play.

"I told you that I would keep you informed." His eyes were now very intent on the road ahead of us.

Unless the person responsible just happens to be your best friend, I thought as I let the lie hang in the air.

To think that some low level Templar stationed over in Barcelona had developed an energy gun that was lethal to all varieties of undead Supernatural was almost funny. That was the first thing Betty told us last night when she'd returned home to my new elven-built fortress that I now called home.

When the name of the person was revealed, Lisa Jenkins, fellow Templar to Race and *my* best friend, let out a little gasp. That was when she filled us in on the fact that Darwin Locke, creator of this terrible weapon, was one of Race's best pals. He had been recruited and trained by Race.

"And how do you know this?" I'd asked Lisa in my best I'm-not-at-all-suspicious voice.

"He was my first sparring partner when I started training," Lisa had replied. "I feel like such an idiot."

"I am sure there is a good reason," Betty said with what might have been sarcasm or fatigue.

"About two weeks before he left for his new post to Spain, I walked in to the gym as he and Race were talking. I guess they didn't hear me." Lisa pinched her lower lip as she dredged up the details. "Darwin said something about Project Omega being ready for testing and wanted to know if Race was still against the idea. Race said something about how this could be seen as the human equivalent of the nuclear option and that it might solidify the entire Supernatural community against the Templar's if the word got out."

"At least he was against the idea of the weapon," Morgan had said flatly after Lisa appeared to be finished.

"So was Oppenheimer," Betty quipped.

The trees parted and up ahead in the massive clearing, my home came into view. I had not been entirely on board with the idea of this fortress being built, but I had to admit…the elves did good work.

On the surface, it looks like a regular home. Well…almost. It looks like a multi-millionaire's regular home. It is a sprawling three-story affair. The driveway is flanked by dense woods for almost a mile before you reach the clearing. There is a massive fountain that the driveway wraps around and there are two small lanes that shoot away from the drive. One of them leads to a six-car garage and the other to a series of small cottages.

I still haven't really seen the entire thing. Seriously, just the upper three stories contain fifteen bedrooms total. It even has circular turrets jutting from all four corners. Then you get to the nine levels below ground and it just becomes a little obscene. The best part about those lower levels is that I don't have to worry about getting hit by sunlight.

Oh, speaking of sunlight, the elves threw in one seriously nice touch. The rooms on the lower levels have what were explained to me as enchanted windows. They look out onto beautiful scenes of nature. The extra cool part is that these are actual places in the world and the windows show those locales basically in real time. The neat part is that it can be sunny and I can stand at the window without being harmed.

Yesterday, I dropped my 'Thank You' card in the mail to Queen Kari. Yeah...an actual and physically tangible card that required a stamp. Remember the days when a trip to the mailbox was not just bills, coupons, local pizza joint flyers and "Have you seen me?' cards? Very few people take the time to send little things like a note expressing thanks these days.

"We're here," Race announced.

"Okay, well..." I did not want us to part ways pissed at each other, but I'm pretty sure he started it. And if he didn't, I bet I can find a way to make it seem like he did if I talk in circles long enough.

"I'll give you a call as soon as the playoff schedule is announced and we know the date of the next game." Race looked at me out of the corner of his eye, but he didn't take his hands off the steering wheel or make any move like he was going to try for a goodnight kiss.

"Fine," I huffed. It didn't look like he was going to open my door for me...he must really be angry. I grabbed the handle and almost broke the damn thing.

"Ava?" he said as I hopped out.

A little too late for that now, fella, I thought as I slammed the door behind me and stomped for the house. I heard the crunch as the tires started rolling. That was a good sign that he was not going to get out and follow me to try and smooth this out.

I held out hope until I heard the van accelerate and head away up the long driveway. Doing my best not to actually stomp my feet, I stormed for the large double-doored entry. I was just reaching the steps that led up to it when the doors both flung open wide and a massive beast stepped forward to almost fill the opening.

"Welcome home, Ava," Theodore the owlbear said in a rumbling voice that held a hint of unease.

Of course, that is not a new tone for the eight-foot-tall creature. For something so large and powerful, he is kind of a wimp. I guess he wasn't treated all that great when he was living under the roof of Claude Mortier, the former Dallas Psychic.

"Thanks, Theo," I said as I climbed the stairs.

I was almost to the top when I noted a problem. I stopped in my tracks and took a step back. My eyes drifted up and down the furred and feathered torso of the owlbear. I had to bite the inside of my check to contain myself and not make the situation any worse than it apparently was.

"I wish you would tell the goblins that the upstairs kitchen is off limits," the big guy said, sounding a lot like Eeyore.

"Have they been watching *Cutthroat Kitchen* again?" I asked, not really needing an answer. There looked to be flour, egg, and something that might be peanut butter (at least I sure hoped so) matted and splattered on Theodore's furry and feathered chest.

"May I go on record as saying that perhaps you should look into what sort of monster this Mr. Alton Brown might be…surely he can't really be human." Theodore stepped aside and ushered me in.

"Nose Wart!" I called.

"Welcome home, Just Ava," a familiar voice called from the kitchen.

A moment later, a dozen goblins filtered into the room. The little herd only got about three steps into the entry foyer when they all froze; looks of what might be fear, if goblins truly feared anything, contorted the dog-like faces.

12

Nose Wart looked down at the hardwood floor and the smeared tracks of whatever was probably all over Theodore and most likely my kitchen. Goopy footprints marked a clear trail back through the open arch.

"What have I said about making messes outside of the goblin warren?" I crossed my arms, jutted out my left hip and began tapping my right foot in my best impersonation of an angry mother.

"The warren is off limits to the males at the moment, Just Ava," Nose Wart replied weakly, a large dollop of something that appeared to have the consistency of quick drying concrete hung from his nose and the wooden spoon in his hand had a gob that could no longer defy gravity as it punctuated his statement with a loud plop when it landed on the floor.

"I don't—" My reprimand was cut off by a scream that made every head turn.

Faster than even my eyes could track, the goblins were gone. All that remained to indicate they'd been here were the tracks that went off in every direction...including up my stairs to the *carpeted* second floor. Somebody or bodies were in a lot of trouble...but at the moment, I had other problems.

That Ghoul Ava Sacks the Quarterback!

2

Walking in your Footsteps

"I know a pack of goblins that are going to be strung up by their toes and beaten like dirty rugs!" a voice shouted from the kitchen.

I shot a glance over at Theodore and saw that he was actually nodding in agreement to the sentiment. I couldn't say that I blamed him...nor was I disagreeing with that possibility as my eyes tore away from the goblin tracks that led up both of the wrap-around staircases that circled the sides of the massive entry area where I still stood. The good news was that I was already over being wrapped up in my emotions regarding Race Mitchell and our little spat.

I headed for the kitchen and physically staggered back a step at what greeted me. You would be hard pressed to tell that all my appliances were brushed stainless steel...or that the counters were a beautiful green granite. Two of my double ovens had smoke wafting from them; and the other two were open wide with large pans of what now resembled charcoal, more than anything else, smoldering on the racks.

"Ever since you told them that they were going to have to learn to cook..." Lisa's voice trailed off as she threw her arms out to indicate the disaster area that was our main kitchen.

"And who told them that Alton Brown was, and I quote,

15

'Amazeballs in the kitchen' and that if they wanted to learn how to cook, they should watch him?" I sniped.

Lisa opened her mouth to retort and was cut off by another voice. "I told you that nothing good would come from trying to civilize those little bastards," Betty scolded as she stepped over a cluster of mixing bowls caked with whatever batter it was that the goblins had attempted to create.

"If they stuck to his regular cooking tips programs like *Good Eats* instead of that horrific game show…which I will re-peat, does not belong on a cooking network any more than *Pawn Stars* does on the History Channel…then things would be fine." Lisa turned to me for support since she knew my feelings on that obscenity that takes up the programming space of quality educa-tional and informative shows.

"Don't look at me." I raised my hands and took an overdra-matic step backwards.

"Way to have my back," Lisa grumbled.

"When did you return?" Betty was apparently finished with the kitchen discussion and turned her attention to me completely.

Betty had gone through some changes while she'd been over in Europe. She'd never been what I would consider a touchy-feely person, but this new version was even more curt and seemed to have very little time for small talk. Also, her hair had turned an absolute snow white and her eyes were in a state of permanent bloodshotedness. (Sorry Mr. Webster, but that is the best description I can give.) Her skin was almost transparent to the point where it looked like somebody had traced her veins in blue Sharpie. So far, she had not offered up a single word about what happened other than the fact that she'd had to take down a coven of witches that were supposedly working with the Tem-plars.

"About five minutes ago," I answered.

"Did loverboy give up his friend yet?" Betty broke into a fit of harsh coughs.

I am pretty sure I saw her wipe blood from the palms of her hands. If she were mortal, I am guessing that she would smell like Thanksgiving Dinner. As it was, it baffled me that I still picked up absolutely no scent from her at all. I've learned that Supernaturals on their death bed emit smells just like any mortal—more or less.

"Nope, and he is on to your return. Somebody ratted you out."

"He's guessing." Betty waved the idea away.

"I don't know why we can't tell him." I slumped down in a chair and winced when something squished under my tush. I reached under my butt and wiped a big goober of goblin-made batter from my jeans.

"Probably the same reason that he hasn't yet told you one of his students is behind the Supernatural Doomsday Death Ray," Betty quipped as she moved past Lisa and took a seat at the breakfast bar.

I opened my mouth to protest, but I had nothing I could say that might counter Betty's fairly ironclad logic. The problem that I was facing was that I really wanted to take my relationship with Race to a new level. I wasn't entirely sure what floor the elevator might stop at, but I was certain that it was past time to get off the ground floor.

"I could always nudge him," Lisa offered.

I glanced over at her and saw what almost might be pity creeping in around the corner of her eyes. The last thing I needed was for somebody to start feeling sorry for me. Not that my love life didn't absolutely qualify as pitiful...having somebody express pity for it was an entirely different matter.

"No, I want him to do this on his own," I said with a shake of my head. Giving Lisa a full up and down look with my eyes, I followed up with a question. "And can I ask where you are off to dressed like that?"

In the past few months, Lisa had undergone a pretty serious fitness regimen. Her body was toned and she had a whole bunch of new and well-defined muscles. I mean...I guess the muscles aren't literally new. I'm sure she has always had them, but now they show up much clearer. Also, she has adopted a jet black that is almost blue for her hair color, and she shaves the sides while keeping the rest just long enough to wear in a ponytail or braid. I was beginning to figure out that the braid meant she was about to go do whatever it is that Templars do. She was wearing a full-body leather cat suit with soft-soled leather boots. She had one-inch spikes at the knees, elbows, and wrists; and the gloves hanging from her belt were basically another weapon to compliment the sword strapped to her back.

"Hogwarts business." Lisa flashed a big smile and gave me a wink. The only problem with the wink was that it implied we were in on some secret together. The truth was that I honestly had no idea where she was off to or what she was up to.

"Can you at least let me know when you think you might be back so I don't go worrying...or at least know when my worrying can begin to feel justified?"

"Actually, I think I should be back within a week to ten days."

The casual way she said that didn't sit well with me. A lot can happen in a week to ten days. And if she got into trouble...

I let that thought die. Lisa had more than proved she was able to handle her business. I lost track on the score as far as who has saved whose ass more. It does not make it any easier to give her space when you factor in the fact that she just turned eighteen.

"Are you going alone on whatever this little mission of yours is?" I pressed lightly.

"Actually..." Lisa paused and put her fingers in her mouth. She let loose with a whistle that would have hurt even my ears if I didn't have enhanced hearing.

I clasped my hands to my head and shot her a nasty look that she totally ignored. Betty did not even seem to have noticed, despite the fact that Lisa was right beside her as opposed to being across the kitchen from me. I was becoming more worried about the uncharacteristically frail looking woman by the minute.

"Yes, Lisa Jenkins?" a voice barked as a goblin skittered into the room, lost his footing on the tile and slid across the floor, slamming into one of the solid oak cupboards with a nasty thud.

"Are you almost ready to go?" Lisa reached down and

picked the goblin up by one arm, setting him down on the floor with surprising gentleness.

"I am prepared and the others are awaiting your departure on the front porch," Belly Ulcer reported.

"Then go join them and I will be along in a moment."

The goblin actually saluted before turning and heading for the front door at a run. I was so taken aback by this formal behavior to somebody that was not me that it took me a moment to realize what was happening. As usual, I apparently did a lousy job of hiding my feelings.

"Don't be mad. I would have asked you, but you have been gone a lot lately and it just seems that our paths have not crossed with enough time for me to ask. I figured that, considering Nose Wart and Belly Ulcer don't get along well, you'd be okay with me taking him and a few of the others with me. If it were Nose Wart, I would have absolutely asked you well in advance," Lisa said in a hurry to forestall my arguments or objections.

"Just try to bring everybody home in one piece."

I walked over and gave my friend a hug. One of the things that I feel I have really learned and internalized these past several months is to never let those I love depart with angry feelings remaining. I have had a few people die on me lately—perhaps not all of them were super close friends—and I don't want to have my conscience eating a hole in me because of some petty squabble. That is more true with Lisa than anybody else I know.

Lisa hugged me back and then headed through the arch and out the door. She was gone about ten seconds when I heard a rattling sound that I initially thought was my brand new sub-zero walk-in conking out. I was only a little surprised when I looked over and connected the harsh rattling sound with Betty.

"Oh, knock it off." Betty made a shooing gesture with her hands. "Looking at me like that is a good way to get slapped."

"So when are you gonna tell me what the hell happened to you?" I took a seat across from her at the breakfast bar and tried once more to get even the slightest hint of a smell from her.

"I was waiting for the child to leave," Betty said with a sigh. As she spoke, I swear that I saw her entire being sort of slump in on itself. It was almost as if she'd shrunk just a little.

"Lisa? You couldn't tell me because of Lisa?"

"Despite the chummy relationship that you two enjoy, I am going to remind you one final time that she is still a Templar...as is that young man you wish to experience in a conjugal manner."

Wow, she sure took all the fun out of my Race fantasies. As for her warnings, I simply did not need them. I did not expect Betty or any of the other Supernaturals to truly understand. They'd lived their entire lives believing a certain thing and it was not realistic to expect them to simply take the word of one of the newest members of the community.

"I promise to be on my guard."

"No you won't." A harsh laugh escaped Betty's lips and she began to cough once more. This time, I was certain that I saw blood fleck her lips.

"So tell me what happened and if there is something that I can do to help," I blurted.

"Get me some brandy first and then I will tell you all you need to know." Betty paused and then a smile carved its way into her face. It looked foreign and strange with as sickly as she was. "Oh, and you can rest assured that there is in fact something I wish you to do...and you will do it."

Unlike when I dealt with Morgan, my reginal Psychic, if Betty told me that I was going to do something, I had no doubts. I also trusted her to give me enough information so that whatever it was she would task me to do could be accomplished with relative ease compared to a Morgan assignment. Morgan was notorious for giving me practically no information and then sending me off on some crazy job where it was always very possible that I would end up dead...for good.

"When I arrived in Spain, I actually believed I would have a little time to catch up with some old friends. Instead, I was immediately met at the airport by the Barcelona and Madrid regions' Psychics. Apparently word had reached them that I was coming and that I was seeking information about that horrible Death Ray device." Betty took the brandy snifter from me and tossed down the entire glass. She tapped the rim and held the empty vessel out to me, obviously signaling for a refill.

"How would—" I started, but Betty held up her hand to silence me as she accepted her brandy and took a sip, closing her eyes and allowing the sounds of pleasure to uncharacteristically escape her lips.

"It is obvious that we have a leak, child. Pay attention." Betty took another sip, this time a bit more subdued in her reaction, and then continued. "In a matter of two days, both of those regions in Spain lost an entire kiss of vampires. The leader of the kiss in Madrid is rumored to be of direct lineage from Vlad Drăculea himself. There was one survivor...a thrall. According to her, three men walked in just after sunset and eliminated the entire kiss. The attack lasted less than two minutes, and only lasted that long because one of the attackers felt it necessary to torture the last vamp before hitting it with the ray gun."

I sat in stunned silence for a moment. Betty was staring at me and I could tell that she was waiting for me to make some sort of connection. That was just another thing that I loved about the woman. She did not expect me to put the pieces together in an instant. She would let me puzzle it out for myself.

There was a flicker...and then it hit me like a ton of bricks. Obviously I am being figurative...but can I just make yet another plea for people to actually look up the meaning of the word 'literal'?

"They came after sunset!" I blurted excitedly.

I had no idea why that was so important, but it did stand out. Betty continued to observe me. I was doing my Winnie-the-pooh impersonation with one finger tapping my temple as I muttered, "Think, think, think." Twice I had to shut down Blodwen as the gwyll attempted to steer me to the answer.

"The natives getting restless?" Betty asked. I looked at her and she locked eyes with me and nodded. Even though she was looking at me, I could tell she was really sort of focused on my head. She knew what lurked in there.

"I got it!" I yelped as I nodded vigorously. "Why would you attack a vampire lair *after* sunset?"

"They wanted to send a message." Betty finished her drink. I gave her a raised eyebrow expression, silently asking if she wanted another refill; she shook her head and set the snifter aside.

I let that sink in. I knew from some of my sparring with Lisa that the Templars were exceptionally trained in the art of combat. Still, a vampire is not something that you mess around with after dark…Templar or not. And as far as taking on an entire kiss. In their lair? That is suicide on the best of days.

"That still doesn't explain what happened to you." I got up and put her glass in the sink. It was sort of like using a thimble to bail out the bilge on the Titanic. That one dirty glass was so insignificant when compared to the disaster that was my kitchen.

"I was just about to get to that," Betty said with a weary sigh.

I didn't want to say it out loud—hell, I barely wanted to admit it to myself—but I was becoming a bit frightened for the woman I had somehow always considered invulnerable. This was just more proof that the Supernaturals are not as immortal as they like to portray.

"I went to check out one of the lairs for myself. In hindsight, perhaps I should have brought along the offered backup. Let that be a lesson to you, Ava. We may think ourselves to be more capable than we truly are. Pride is a knife waiting to cut you down." Betty paused for a moment as if hearing something distant, and then continued. "I was in the basement sifting through the little piles of diamond dust where all the vamps had fallen. It was evident that the ones responsible held vampires in no regard at all as many of the piles were kicked apart, trampled through, or both.

"When I discovered the lockbox sitting on a table, I knew that this was solely about hatred. All the valuables that the kiss kept were still inside including a necklace that should easily fetch a few hundred thousand."

Betty reached inside her shirt and pulled out the most exquisite diamond and sapphire necklace I'd ever seen in my life. The smallest of diamonds would have been almost gaudy if used as the stone for an engagement ring.

"I was on my way back upstairs when a pair of large men appeared at the top of the stairs. They mistook me for a vamp, saying that they were so glad I'd come home to discover all the other blood-sucking abominations—their words, not mine— reduced to the piles of dirt they truly were. I let them think they were right, and one of them drew the ray gun from a ridiculously large holster on his hip. The beam hit me square in the chest. The looks on their faces when I glanced down at where I'd been shot and then back up at them…priceless. Perhaps it was my fault for how this played out. Now I was the one who acted out of arrogance."

She went into the details of a fight that involved her casting spells that I'd never heard of, much less knew she was capable of performing. She blasted one guy with ice crystals. Supposedly it would be the equivalent of taking a round of bird shot from a shotgun at relatively close range. The ice melts leaving no evidence, but the results are fatal when that blast hits a person square in the face.

"I had no idea that the Templars were taking werebears," Betty said, her statement sounding like a mixture of bemusement and concern. "When that boy caught me with his grizzly-sized paw, I thought that I was done for. If not for that surviving thrall following me and knowing where a silver sword was hanging on a bedroom wall, an incredibly convoluted series of coincidences by the way, I would have likely died in that basement."

"The thrall saved you?"

"Came in and lopped that werebear's head right off," Betty managed to laugh around another series of raspy coughs. "Unfortunately, the poison of the lycanthropic disease has gotten into my blood. It is just too much for my system to handle."

I was afraid to speak now. I mean, this sounded like she was going to die.

"So I need you to do me a favor."

I shook my head when it registered to me that Betty was speaking to me…asking me for a favor. I began to have my suspicions as to what those might be and my head was already wagging back and forth.

"I'm not ready to leave yet, Ava. The war is finally here, and I will not miss it because of some werebear that got in a lucky shot." Betty sat up straight. Her bloodshot eyes appeared to whiten and her skin regained some of its natural pallor. "Besides, you need me. Blodwen is an excellent advisor, but between the two of us, your knowledge would be increased exponentially."

"I just don't think I can eat you, Betty."

I realize that statement could be taken a number of ways if taken out of context. I know that just saying it out loud made me start to giggle. Betty made it worse when she said one simple word.

"Phrasing."

The two of us looked at each other for a moment and then we started laughing like crazed fiends. I saw tears rolling down her cheeks and knew that she had to be feeling a lot of stress if this release was so drastic. Betty is not the type to laugh hysterically.

In case you are scratching your head and wondering what the hell is so funny, I will say one word: *Archer*. If you have not watched this animated series, you have my pity. Betty and I stumbled across it by accident one night and had to go back and find the entire series on Netflix so that we could binge watch. That should tell you how funny it was if Betty binge watched six entire seasons over two days.

"I'm dying, Ava," Betty finally said after we managed to laugh ourselves out. "If you finish me, you will be doing me a favor. Then you just tuck in and enjoy."

"But I just can't go and kill you," I insisted.

"You won't be killing me, Ava. If you do this, you will allow me to continue on..." Betty's voice faded for a second and then she leaned forward. Her voice took on a conspiratory tone when she continued. "And just imagine the power you will add to your arsenal."

And now you know why the female ghouls were hunted, Blodwen's voice echoed in my head.

"It feels wrong," I whined. Seriously, for whatever reason, I was very uncomfortable with this scenario.

"I told you when we began and I started offering you all this information that Morgan kept from you that there would eventually be a price." Betty let that statement hang in the air for several seconds. "Nothing is free. Ava."

"That's not fair."

"Life...and death...they aren't fair, but they happen every single day."

"Are you sure there is nothing that can be done?"

"Don't you think that I have exhausted all those possibilities? Do you truly believe that I want to leave this physical world?" She broke into more coughs and then looked at me with a bloody-toothed smile. "And do you for one moment believe that I want to live inside that head of yours?"

I sighed, my head dropping in submission. "I'll do it."

"I know." My head popped up and I saw Betty had moved right in front of me. "I am just glad you finally agreed to do this on your own."

I didn't like how she said that. Something was fishy. The wave of deliciousness that hit me was so thick that it made me stagger back a few steps.

"I've been shielding," Betty explained as she hobbled over and stood nose-to-nose with me now. "If you would not have agreed, then I would have taken the choice from you."

Sharkmouth was on and my fingers and toes had gone switch. I was already back on my feet and was holding Betty in my hands, her feet several inches off the ground.

"Do it!" Betty barked.

My claws slashed and cut her in two. I don't think she even had a chance to cry out. A very small voice in the back of my head that I was only mostly sure belonged to me insisted that severing her spine like that had made the death painless. I think that is something that we do to make ourselves feel better...say that somebody died a painless death. I mean, do we really know that dying in your sleep is such a good thing? If you have experienced the degree of nightmares that I have, would you really want that to be your last experience in this world? Maybe that person died because it was their worst nightmare ever…and the heart couldn't take it.

Unlike some of the other instances where I have consumed a powerful Supernatural, I didn't blackout. I was pondering the reason when a familiar voice chirped from inside my head, *That is why I had you pour me a few stiff drinks. The booze mellowed the effects.*

Clever.

I didn't get this old without having a bit going on upstairs.

Hmm, then I might not be around so long after all, I pined inwardly.

Don't sell yourself short, child, Blodwen piped up. *You are a much brighter person than you give yourself credit.*

Tell that to Morgan.

Believe it or not, she is more than aware of your mental abilities, Betty answered. *You have amazed her time after time with your ability to figure things out on the fly.*

She sure doesn't act like it.

She is walking a very fine line right now, Ava, Betty said, her tone becoming almost motherly. Not like my mother…but like a warm, loving, caring mother. *She thinks that giving you too much information might hamper your thinking process. She wants you to stay sharp. The tip of the iceberg is all we've really seen in this coming war.*

That wasn't very comforting.

3

This is How We Do It

The knock at the door came at exactly 9:30 PM. I already knew who it was, so I didn't bother peeking at the security monitor as I walked up the hall to answer it.

"Come in, Anthony." I made a sweeping gesture with my arm and stepped back to allow the behemoth to enter.

"Oh. Em. Gee," a voice squealed.

Anthony was shoved aside as a waif of a girl barged past and planted herself directly in front of me. She was maybe a shade over four feet tall and had emerald green hair. That was offset by her golden skin tone. Not tan, I actually mean gold as in Fort Knox. Her eyes were a vibrant purple and the lashes fluttered like butterfly wings as she gawked at me. She was not busty, but there were definitely some feminine curves. Her waist was sickeningly small, but she had some serious J-Lo booty following her around.

Water elf, both Blodwen and Betty said in unison.

"She *is* a real live ghoul," the waif squealed again, clapping her hands for emphasis and then tucking them under her chin as she made moon eyes at me.

Since I knew that my company was aware of my true nature, I'd skipped the spray tan. My only attempt at concealing my identity were the dark shades that I wore. I'd found that wearing them made many of the Supernaturals under my roof feel a lot more at ease. I guess there is something about solid black orbs staring at you that can be a bit unnerving.

"Please excuse Kayleeni," Anthony apologized, shooting a murderous glare at the girl who appeared oblivious to his discomfort. "I told her that she would be sent back to the car if she gets too annoying."

"Have you eaten anything cool yet?" Kayleeni blurted.

"Okay, that's it!" Anthony bellowed.

"Wait a minute." I raised a hand. The half-troll paused, but he shot daggers from his eyes at the water elf. "Are you some kind of ghoul nut?" I directed my question at the girl.

She puzzled over my statement for a few seconds and then appeared to understand. "You even use modern day slang...so you have to be a relatively recent turn." Anthony elbowed her in the side and she shook her head as if to clear it. "I have been studying all the old legends ever since I can remember. I just never thought I would meet one...much less a female. You are supposed to be—"

"Extinct," I said for her.

"But obviously you aren't," Kayleeni chirped. "You have the classic gray skin, and I bet your teeth and nails are something to behold. Also, I am willing to bet that you have the ebony eyes behind those dark shades."

I tipped the glasses down to the end of my nose. As soon as she saw them, she practically danced a jig.

"I think I like her," I stage-whispered to Anthony.

"Yes, well I don't want to keep you, Miss Birch." Anthony swept the petite girl aside and took a spot directly in front of me. "I came here hoping that I could hire you to take care of something for me."

"And what would a great big guy like you need a girl like me for?" My comment made Kayleeni giggle. When Anthony turned to glare, she covered her mouth with both hands.

"As you know, the team made the playoffs."

I stared dumbly for a moment. With all that had gone on in the past twenty-four hours, I'd all but forgotten about the local indoor football league team. I smacked my forehead and nodded for him to continue.

"Well, a few weeks ago, I was at a clan gathering—"

"Say what?" I coughed.

Anthony shook his head and then touched his arm as if bringing my attention to the color of his skin. "A troll clan gathering. We have them twice a year. It is sort of a chance for us to all gather together and check in. It is also where the females select their mates."

That sounded interesting, but I did not interrupt him with stupid questions. Maybe when my job was over I could get Anthony to clue me in on the troll culture. For now, I needed to focus on my potential client and hear what his needs might be.

"During the gathering, a troll by the name of Gilbert Jones came up to me."

"Gilbert Jones?" I let the dubiousness that I felt come dripping through in my voice. "A troll named Gilbert?"

"Many of us who have melded into your society have taken up human names. It would not do to keep our troll names. Most are not pronounceable by the human tongue."

He's right, Betty agreed. *I met a troll once. I thought he had some sort of stomach disorder, turns out he was just trying to introduce himself to me.*

"Okay. I'll give Gilbert a pass on his name," I said, forcing the laughter out of my voice.

"Anyways," Anthony now looked like he was beginning to regret coming here, "he told me that Lavontra had made her decision on who she would select as a mate. I just figured that he was coming to rub it in. Turns out, she said that she would marry whichever one of us won the championship."

"So then I take it Gilbert plays football as well?"

"Yes, he is the center for the Arizona team."

"Okay, well, I still don't see what that has to do with me. I love my team and all…you guys are super. But I won't do something dirty to keep Gilbert from playing, so if that is why you came, you are wasting your time."

"Actually, I am kinda glad that you feel that way," Anthony

admitted with a little sigh that might've been relief. "Because I would never do something to tarnish the good name of the sport." He swallowed big and I noticed Kayleeni elbow the much larger man in the ribs.

"Tell her…I bet she takes the job."

"You are obviously aware of our quarterback since you seem to be an actual fan of the team?" Anthony began hesitantly.

Colt Faber. I want you to picture the prototypical all-American male with a hint of mischief gleaming from the eyes, and that is Colt Faber. The team program has him listed at six and a half feet tall and two hundred and twenty pounds. He has blond hair kept in a GQ style with one lock that is just too perfectly placed down his forehead and brushing just above his eyes to be an accident. Those eyes are a crystal blue, and he has a dimple on his chin that makes him all that much cuter.

"Please tell me he is human," I gulped as my brain tried to leap ahead to whatever it was that Anthony was going to ask of me.

"He's very human," Anthony replied. "And that is why he is in so much danger. Gilbert has sworn to kill him. It is no secret that Colt's arm is our most lethal weapon. His degree of accuracy has gotten him a second look by the pros. We probably lose him at the end of the year. But if we lose him now, our chances of winning the championship are basically gone."

"And the whole thing about Colt being dead would suck too," I added with an undisguised tone of derision.

"Of course," Anthony blurted. "I thought that went without saying."

"The value of a person's life should never simply be taken for granted," I scolded. I let him stew over that for a moment before I continued. "And so I am assuming that you want me to talk to this Gilbert and convince him that killing Colt would be a bad idea."

"Not exactly." Anthony turned to Kayleeni and gave a curt nod. She rushed out my front door, leaving it wide open. Just as I was about to question as to whether or not her conception and/or birth had taken place in a barn, she returned with, you guessed it, Colt Faber. An obviously confused Colt Faber to be exact.

"I want you to be his bodyguard." Anthony practically yanked Colt off his feet to present him to me.

"Say what?" I practically choked. "You mean like Kevin Costner and Whitney Houston? What would make you even remotely think that I am qualified...better yet, even sort of interested in being a bodyguard?"

"The owner of the team is willing to pay you a hundred grand per week for as long as we last in the playoffs...and the Troll Preservation Society will match it."

"Okay." Those were pretty good reasons; I'd give him that. "But, and please don't be offended by this, Mr. Faber, why would anybody pony up that kinda money for somebody to basically babysit a grown man for a couple of weeks?"

Yeah, I know. I just pitched a fit about the value of a human life, and here I was trying to have somebody quantify Colt's. Does that make me a hypocrite?

"The threat will be over as soon as our season ends...one way or another. Also, apparently the team is in talks with a very famous local shoe distributor. Winning a championship could net a massive sponsorship," Anthony replied.

"So this is not as much about keeping Mr. Faber alive as it is making sure that the owners can score a big payday." I could understand that logic.

I can feel you scratching your head at my apparent hypocrisy. Before you go getting all indignant, ask yourself how often you do something based on finances. People say that money can't buy happiness. Maybe not, but it can sure rent it for a while. One of the biggest issues that tear married folks apart is finances. Sorry, that is the world we live in.

"I'll take the job." I glanced at Colt and then back to Anthony. "And can I assume that Mr. Faber here has some degree of knowledge in regards to those who wish him harm as well as who I am and why you are offering me this gig?"

"He said you're a ghoul," Colt laughed. "And this troll thing is hilarious. I guess the big guys need something to make themselves feel special. Linemen seldom get the press that the skill players do when it comes to football."

I turned to the handsome, boyish looking athlete. As soon as I was certain that I had his attention, I took off my glasses. I waited for his inevitable reaction. He just stared at me with a blank expression.

"Still not convinced?" I gasped.

"Contacts. I bet those set you back a few hundred bucks. I have a pair with a target design that I wore for my photo shoot. They let me keep them after as a gift. I asked the makeup girl and she said they were almost a grand!" Colt smiled at me and made like he was yawning.

An idea hit and I weighed out just how much trouble I might get in. Of course several other ideas tried to work their way to the front...ideas that would likely not get me in trouble if Morgan found out, but the way that Colt was so obviously skeptical felt a bit like a challenge.

I heard Betty and Blodwen protest when I apparently broadcast my idea inwards. As fast as possible, I locked them away before they could talk sense into me.

"Come with me." I motioned to the door that would lead down to my own personal food locker.

We entered a large room with a massive stainless steel table in the center. On the far wall was the door to a walk in refrigerator that was larger than most peoples' living rooms. On massive shelves were my assortment of relatively fresh corpses.

"Whoa," Colt breathed as he stepped inside with me.

I felt Anthony close on our heels. His cough of disapproval was tuned out just as fast as I'd shut down Blodwen and Betty.

"No way," Kayleeni blurted.

I walked over to the closest body. The curse of needing to eat within every twelve-hour period was still keeping me in its grip. Perhaps I should hire myself to solve that little mystery...someday. For now, it was feeding time for this little gray ghoul.

"Those can't be real," Colt scoffed, but I could see as well as hear the conviction slipping in his belief that this is all some big charade.

"Go ahead and check them out." I ushered him past me and watched as he wandered from one corpse to another. For whatever good it did him, he poked and prodded one body and then the next. After the fifth or sixth one, he turned to look at me. "Is this some branch of the morgue or something?"

Funny thing about humans…they don't like being confused. Their mind will do everything in its power to make sense out of things. That is actually part of the natural defense keeping the Supernatural community safe.

I walked up beside Colt and willed Sharkmouth into being. When he turned to face me, his eyes went wide and he staggered back a few steps. The whites of his eyes seemed to double in size.

"No, these are actual corpses that never made it to the morgue. Most of them were homeless men and women who simply died and would not be missed by a system that really doesn't care that much about them." I let my switch-fingers pop out and ran one bladed digit down the chest of what had once been a man with hopes and dreams.

"B-b-but you can't be…" Colt's words fizzled on his tongue and faded as he stared in open-mouthed disbelief.

I started to feed and barely noticed when the young man's eyes rolled back in his head and he fainted. It would have been funny if not for the fact that I'd just revealed my true nature to a regular human.

"Are you crazy?" Anthony snapped, scooping Colt into his arms.

"Some would say yes," I spoke after gulping down an entire arm, my crazy sharp teeth making short work of the stringy meat and brittle bones.

"That is so cool," Kayleeni squeaked as she moved around to get a better view as I ate.

"You didn't seem too shy about throwing around your status as a troll," I shot back around a mouthful of leg. "Besides, if I am going to be protecting this guy, he needs to know that I am no joke."

"Mission accomplished," Kayleeni chortled.

"Tell your bosses that I will take the job. I want half up front. Non-refundable no matter the outcome." I considered things a moment and then added, "Also, I will need seats in the front row and full access to anything or anyplace the players will be."

"That shouldn't be a problem from the owners of the team. I doubt the Troll Preservation Society will be as generous." Anthony headed up the stairs with Colt slung over his shoulder. "I can show myself out so that you can finish...*eating*. Somebody will be by tomorrow with your retainer."

I watched the big half-troll and the water elf exit. Kayleeni glanced back once and gave me a freakishly big smile before waving and closing the door behind her. I consumed the rest of my little feast. Once I was done, I consciously focused on letting Blodwen and Betty back out to roam the caverns of my mind.

That was just plain foolish, Betty started in right away. *You can be sentenced to death if you allow the humans to know of us with such careless tactics.*

For one, I am already on somebody's hit list. Then there is the whole thing where you people keep saying that I could be the one to lead the Supernatural community into the light or some such nonsense. I paused and waited for a rebuttal. When none seemed to be forthcoming, I continued. *Besides, that kid ain't saying a thing. He plans on playing in the big leagues. How long before he starts spewing about ghouls and that sort of thing before they put him in one of those jackets with the long sleeves that tie in the back?*

You are playing a dangerous game, Ava, Betty snapped. *If Morgan finds out, she might just sign the contract to take you out herself.*

I chuckled. I tried to picture Morgan facing off with me. I'd consumed a Psychic. Other than being able to detect when another Supernatural enters my district—which I'd already handed over to one of Morgan's pals—I had not felt any new powers trying to express themselves.

That brought another thought to my head. As I ventured

down into some of the lower levels of my fortress, I decided that I was going to get something out of consuming Betty. Besides, if I was going to have to take on a full -blooded troll, I wanted to stack my arsenal. I'd mixed it up with trolls before, and you never know how adept this one might be at fighting.

So, Betty, remember that nifty little spell that you cast? The one that was like electric ice?

That Ghoul Ava Sacks the Quarterback!

4

Somebody's Watching Me

I wiped the flecks of frost from my fingers and answered my phone. I know people keep saying that land lines are history, but I would like to see a cell get reception down here in the fifth level below the ground.

"Hello?" I huffed. The frustration I felt about not being able to get Betty's little spell down to a useable weapon coming across clear in my tone.

So far, I'd shot a block of ice about the size of a Chihuahua across the room. It didn't even have enough momentum to chip or crack…until it hit the floor at least. Basically it was like a slow-pitch softball offering. The most damage it would do would happen if it landed on your toes. Once, a ball of what I thought was electric energy came from my hands, but it popped out of existence less than two feet away. So, a mugger would have a nasty surprise, but anybody much past arms' reach would remain unscathed.

"Did I catch you at a bad time?" a swarthy voice rumbled in my ear.

Instantly I felt my tummy tingle. I know that Race and I didn't part on the best of terms after our last date, but that did not reduce the amount of hormonal raging that was taking place in my mommy regions.

"No…just trying out some new weapons. I just can't seem to get the hang of it is all." I put my back against the wall and slid to the floor. It was like high school all over again…almost.

"You know I can give you a few lessons if you are ever up for it."

"I might take you up on that someday." He'd likely be useless when it came to helping me with anything I learned from Betty or some of the other entities living inside my head, but maybe he could give me some cool hand-to-hand skills.

"Anyway, I called about the next game, it is—"

"Next Friday," I blurted. "And why don't you see what you can get for your tickets, maybe use the money to buy me something pretty?"

"Umm…" I could hear the utter confusion in his tone.

"What if I told you that I scored us tickets in the front row and at midfield?"

"I'd ask you who you ate that had tickets in their pockets? They've been sold out for the last three home games of the season and from what I heard, the tickets for this game actually sold out twenty minutes after they went on sale."

"Yeah, well if you just got hired as the bodyguard for Colt Faber by the team's owner, you get a few perks."

The line was silent for a moment. I was waiting for the excitement…the gratitude.

"What have you gotten yourself into, Ava?"

Okay, I was not expecting that. He actually sounded a bit miffed.

"Just what I said," I answered hesitantly. "Jeez, if you don't wanna go with me and sit in the front row, then don't. I'll ask somebody else."

"Actually, the seats sound amazing," Race came back sounding much too cheerful. Now I was on my guard.

"And they are mine for the duration of the playoffs." He didn't need to know that Colt's murder would put an end to the choice seats. Besides, I figured that any attempts on our star quarterback would come outside of the playing field.

We made plans to meet for dinner the night of the game. It

wasn't that we didn't try to set up something before then; unfortunately, our schedules just did not allow for it. That meant I would be getting better acquainted with the shower massage. Seriously, Race needed to close this deal soon.

I hung up the phone and went back to practicing Betty's electric ice spell. By the time darkness fell and I was able to go to the upper floors, I'd not really improved much. At one point, I accused Betty of withholding something from me.

Why would I do that? the woman had snapped.

She had a point. I was simply frustrated. I apologized.

That's quite alright, child, she said comfortingly. *If magic was easy, everybody would do it.*

Heading upstairs, I ran into Nose Wart. He was waiting for me in a gleaming kitchen that was so clean you could probably eat off the floor. You're probably thinking that is a tired statement and that nobody would actually do that. Well, you haven't ever lived with goblins. Plus, I eat corpses, so it isn't like I have a lot of room to cast stones.

A female goblin was sitting next to the archway that led to the entry hall. I was getting pretty good at reading the little creatures and this one was visibly nervous. I didn't recognize her, but in all honesty, other than Nose Wart; most of them really do look a lot alike unless I know them well enough on a personal level to be able to pick them out.

"I have completed the cleaning evolution of the entire kitchen area, Just Ava. I hope it is to your satisfaction." Nose Wart made a low bow and I went on my guard.

Ever since our little adventure together, we'd come to a bit of an understanding. He was still polite and treated me as his leader, but the reverence and simpering had been drastically reduced.

"Okay, Nose Wart, spill it. What are you not telling me?"

The female goblin rose to her feet and came to stand beside the flustered looking male. She kept her gaze on the floor, but I caught her peeking up at me and then shooting a glance at the goblin beside her.

"I have chosen a new mate," Nose Wart announced.

For the first time since she'd vanished from my consciousness, I was glad Butt Pimple wasn't present. The presence that had declared herself as Boudicca had snatched her and retreated to some corner of my mind and sealed herself away. I'd been given the ultimatum to do a mind walk and come in to face the being that is supposedly the first female ghoul in history. I was all ready to go, but Blodwen, Betty, and Morgan talked me out of it saying that basically it would be like a modern day grade school kid picking a fight with a Roman gladiator.

I was willing to hold off for now, but I was pretty certain that the time would come when I was going to have to face off with her. I'd been trying to do some research on Boudicca, but it wasn't very encouraging. Also, when I shared with Morgan some of what the history books recounted about her…well…she laughed. Morgan doesn't laugh. Ever.

"I am heavy with his litter and hope to give him many brave sons." The female goblin stepped up to me and clasped her belly with both hands. It was sort of roundish, but then again, so were most goblins' bellies.

"Also, Just Ava, I have come to request that you give us permission to rename our clan to something more suitable." Nose Wart edged past the female again and now stood directly in front of me, staring up with his big rheumy eyes.

"One thing at a time, Nose Wart." I held up my hand like a traffic cop. "Maybe you could tell me this new mate's name?"

"You honor me by asking, Just Ava." The female once again stepped forward. Maybe it was me, but the female goblin seemed a bit pushy. I wasn't sure I liked her all that much.

"Her name is Teat Mucous," Nose Wart answered proudly. "She was a rival of my late Butt Pimple. They fought on three occasions and each time it was a no contest as both of them lost consciousness from blood loss."

"How…wonderful?"

"And so do I have your consent to change our name? We wish to honor you and hope that you will do us this one favor."

"Sure, why not," I said with a shrug of my shoulders.

"Excellent. Then from now on we shall be known as Just

Goblins."

It took me a second to understand exactly what Nose Wart had said. My original thought was that they would simply be goblins. Nothing fancy. Then I realized that Nose Wart still believed my name to be Just Ava from one of our earliest meetings when he'd called me by some honorific or another and I told him my name was just Ava. He took that to mean my name was *Just* Ava.

"You are now the Just Goblins clan?" I asked a bit too excited.

"If you find that acceptable." Nose Wart squeezed his eyes shut as if he expected me to smack him in the head.

"I think that is a fantastic name, Nose Wart. I approve wholeheartedly." That was more than I could say about his new squeeze. For whatever reason, I just was not cool with Butt Pimple being replaced so quickly.

This is that whole thinking like a human thing that we keep scolding you about, Betty piped up. *Most goblins seek another mate before they have even digested their last one.*

I had forgotten about the fact that goblins actually taste-tested their potential mate to ensure compatibility and then apparently consume them upon death. I'd actually been the one to eat Nose Wart's last mate after a nasty fight with a lamia.

"So, when can I expect to hear the pitter patter of little goblin feet?" I asked.

"By the next full moon," Teat Mucous replied.

"Super." I resisted the urge to pat Nose Wart on the head and instead tossed him a hasty and sloppy salute. "Well, the kitchen looks great, so I guess…carry on."

***

I watched the team come out of the tunnel as they began to partake in their pre-game warm-up rituals. My eyes were locked on Colt as he found a spot on the far side of the field and began to throw short passes to a few of his receivers. I also saw Anthony Riddle standing in a cluster of big men. They smacked each other's shoulder pads and then began to go through a series of stretches. I had never really paid attention to this activity. I had to admit that I was more than a little impressed as I watched some of these men fold and bend themselves in ways that I wouldn't dream of.

"These are really great seats," Race leaned into me and whispered.

"I know, right?" I beamed at Race. I had a giddy feeling in my belly. He was leaning forward and looked like a kid at Christmas. I could tell that he was seriously enjoying himself.

I scanned the other team and allowed myself to focus. This wasn't the squad that Gilbert the Troll played for, but Anthony had shown me what to look for. More specifically, he told me what to *smell* for. None of the other team offered up the aroma that screamed troll. I was thinking that I might be able to just sit back and enjoy the game with Race. Maybe I'd even get lucky tonight.

I seriously needed a win in that department. Yesterday I'd intentionally overloaded the washing machine and sat on it while I waited for the spin cycle.

I looked around as the arena began to fill up. According to the marquee out front, the game was sold out. It was still an hour until kickoff, but the place was almost half full and there was a buzz of excitement in the air.

Until recently, I'd never really been to a major league sporting event that captured my attention. I'd watched a few games in high school. I'd even been to a few major league baseball games, but I find watching baseball to be a massive bore. The thing is, I went with the mindset that I wasn't going to have fun. I refused to allow myself to care.

If you have only experienced a professional sporting event on television, then you don't know what you're missing…and you have my pity. There really is nothing like it in the world. Things are so much faster in person.

Sort of like assassination attempts apparently.

I was sitting in my seat just enjoying the sights and sounds when I caught a glimpse of something. At first I wasn't sure I'd seen anything at all; sort of like when you think you see something flash by out of the corner of your eye.

I locked my senses in and gave that area another more detailed look and was frustrated when I still didn't see anything. I stood up and leaned on the waist high padded wall that surrounded the playing field. I was just about to write it off to nerves or just all the excitement and activity.

Then I saw them.

A trio of goblins were climbing over the wall at the far end of the field. One of them got tangled up in the nets that stretch across the entire end zone. Since goblins are apparently not visible to the human eye, nobody noticed the other two scurry back to get their cohort free. All it looked like was the net sort of wavering—perhaps from the air conditioning.

"What is it, Ava?" Race had gotten to his feet and was now looking around, but doing his best to make it seem casual.

"Goblins." I gave a slight nod at the trio as they now began stumping towards where Colt continued to warm up

Race looked over to where I'd indicated. As a Templar, he had no trouble seeing them. I felt him tense and his hand went reflexively to his hip.

"I can handle this," I whispered to Race.

I was pleased to see that Anthony had done as I'd instructed. As soon as I waved both hands over my head like I was greeting a friend across the field, he moved over to Colt and prompted him to head for the locker room.

I scooted past Race and headed up the stairs for the main concourse. As I walked, I tugged the lanyard hanging around my neck from under my blue and gray team jersey. I was really digging the fact that gray was one of our team's primary colors. I'd been able to skip having my skin airbrushed.

I waded through all the fans, a few whooping and giving me a thumbs-up. I am pretty sure it is the gray skin. They probably think I am really into demonstrating my love of the team.

I reached the stairs heading down to the bowels of the arena and increased my speed. As I held up my all-access badge for the security person, I only briefly wondered what they really thought an elderly lady would be able to do if a serious issue were to arise.

I rounded the corner just as Anthony and Colt emerged from the tunnel from the field entrance. I broke into a fast jog to catch them.

"What is it?" Anthony rumbled.

"Goblins," I answered. "I saw three of them climb over the wall at the far end of the field."

"You sure they were here for Colt?"

"See many goblins here at the games this season?" I shot back.

"We've come for the man-child!" a voice squeaked from back up the tunnel that led to the field.

Anthony and I both turned to the voice but Colt remained oblivious and mostly looked annoyed. Being Supernaturals, we had no problem seeing not three, but what was now a small pack of the little dog-faced creatures. They were all brandishing a variety of weapons that looked to be assembled from scraps of what might've once been actual swords, knives, and such.

I instinctively pushed both men behind me and advanced on the little group. A quick count told me there were seventeen of them.

"I don't usually give warnings," I hissed. "You can turn around and run for your lives...or you die here."

Ever since Boudicca's essence or whatever the hell it was living in my head had made itself known, I'd felt this surge of power and what was almost like a need to commit violence. In two steps, Sharkmouth was present and I kicked off my slip on shoes. Next, I willed my switch-digits into being and brought my arms out wide to display them.

There was a moment's pause where I thought that just maybe these fearless bits of walking fodder were going to withdraw. That was quickly washed away when one of them let out a howl and charged at me with his rusty blade held high.

"Get Colt into the locker room," I called over my shoulder as I braced myself for the first goblin.

"I can help!" Anthony shouted back.

"Do what I said!" I ordered as my hand came across and removed the first head.

"What the hell is going on?" Colt yelled. The poor guy sounded absolutely confused.

I heard the door shut as three more of the vermin reached me. Two were females, but I could sort that out in my mind later. I swung with both hands and my left actually cleaved both of them in half at around their waists.

There is nothing to sort out, Betty's voice consoled. *This is a fight and they will not see you as anything other than the obstacle keeping them from their target. In war, soldiers are not men and women...they are simply enemy combatants.*

I spun with a roundhouse kick and tore apart another goblin. Something pressed on my right side and I glanced down just long enough to see the shaft of a three-foot-long spear jutting from my body. I grabbed it and ripped it out. With a flick of my wrist, I hurled it at a goblin brandishing a small axe with a nasty hook on the back side of the head. It caught the tiny creature in the throat. I probably couldn't have hit it there if I'd aimed, but the results were spectacular as it tumbled back into some of its pals and sent three of them to the ground in a heap.

I jumped and landed in the midst of the chaos. Using the switch-toes, I did a little pawing at the floor like a bull and shredded the pile of goblins before any of them had the chance to recover.

Apparently that was enough. Only four remained. I didn't think I'd taken down thirteen, but I guess it is hard to keep track when you are just flailing around wildly.

"We submit, Ghoul Mother!" one of the goblins wailed, throwing itself on the floor, face down in submission.

The others followed suit and I paused. I wanted to make sure that I was on the right path, so I figured I would fire off a question.

"Were you sent by Gilbert the Troll?" I asked.

There was a chorus of confirmations. That was actually a relief. Up until this point, I was taking a job based on somebody's account of the situation. That could have been an absolute bag of manure.

"I want you to go back to him with a message." I leaned down and plucked one of the goblins from the floor. With no effort at all, I brought it up so that its face was level with mine. With my other hand I tipped my dark shades to the end of my nose. "Tell Gilbert that Colt is under my protection and that if he continues in his attempts to kill Colt Faber, I will cease just being Colt's personal bodyguard. I will actively hunt down Gilbert and feast on him like he's a Thanksgiving turkey."

I dropped the goblin and it scurried over to the others. Like rats fleeing a sinking ship, they all turned tail and scampered back up the tunnel. At that moment, the team was returning from their warm-ups. With the slightest thought, I brought back my nails and reigned in Sharkmouth.

The goblins had scampered up the tunnel and directly into the path of the approaching mob of football payers. I saw one of the goblins pick the wrong path and end up being trampled underfoot as the players jogged along. One of the fellas sort of stumbled and then looked around. A few of his buddies gave him grief about not being very graceful.

If you've ever just been out walking and trip over nothing, chances are actually pretty good that you just tripped over a goblin. They are drawn to the vents of your dryer and often come seeking a lone sock. Many of the males like to wear them over their naughty parts as a decoration. At least now you know where that one missing sock probably ended up. It isn't as much of a mystery once you've seen a goblin sporting his pilfered laundry item. I know that I used to think I was going crazy. How many times had I tossed in a load of laundry and then pulled them out of the dryer to fold only to discover I was one sock short?

I hurried back to the corridor and cleared the way for the team as they all hustled to the locker room. Taking up the rear was the coaching staff. I could hear them complaining about the sudden departure of their star quarterback.

"...gets an offer from the pros and already he is acting like a fucking prima donna," one large man with an even larger belly complained angrily.

After slipping back into my shoes, I headed back to my seats and smiled when I spotted Race. He'd purchased one of the giant foam swords and shields and was whipping up our section with some rousing and rather creative chants. That told me one thing: he knew that I could handle myself and he was not concerned.

I joined him, a large and very over-priced beer in my hand. I handed it to Race and he kissed me.

Both of us sort of froze. Even though it was really brief, that was our first actual kiss. I smiled when a hint of red crept around the tops of his ears.

Leaning close, I whispered, "Play your cards right and there could be a lot of firsts crossed off the list tonight."

I turned and plopped down in my seat leaving the brawny, self-assured Templar looking like a fish out of water. His mouth opened and closed at least three times before he finally shut it and sat down beside me.

He turned to say something and just as he opened his mouth, the arena lights dimmed and the sounds, flames, and lasers announced the beginning of team introductions. Whatever he was about to say was drowned by the capacity crowd rising almost in unison and screaming at the top of its lungs. I was one of that crowd. A moment later, Race was beside me, hands clapping in time to the beat.

The opponents from Des Moines came out and were greeted by lusty boos and cat calls. Some television reality show song contest winner came out to sing the Star Spangled Banner—she wasn't terrible.

Once the game started, I discovered that I had a difficult time keeping an eye on what was happening on the field and the charge left under my protection. Of course, when he was on the field, he had every eye in the place on him.

By halftime, it was clear that the team from Des Moines was not anywhere close to being up to the task of playing the spoiler. We held a five touchdown lead. That allowed me to slip out of my seat and head back to the tunnel where I'd killed the goblins.

All that remained of the dead were little dark smears on the concrete floor. Even their little weapons had been ground into dust. I toed a bit of the debris as I walked down the tunnel to where the players would all be congregating during the game.

Just as I was about to head back, I caught a very strong whiff of rocks. I turned expecting to see Anthony coming up the corridor. It just did not dawn on me that he would be in the locker room doing whatever it is that football players do in between halves of the game.

"Ava Birch," a massive hulk of a creature rumbled.

When I say massive, I mean this thing almost completely filled the hall. His head looked like a BB on a massive set of shoulders that actually rubbed the walls of this tunnel. Whatever sort of troll this was—and I was going off of smell at the moment—it had a skin tone similar to mine. Its slate gray color was broken up by patches of greenish-brown that almost looked like moss. The face, as small as it was, had close set eyes that were also a shade of gray in pools of red. The nose made me think of Jimmy Durante…or at least the cartoon version of him. It had warts all over it as did the rest of the skin I could see. It wore what looked like a bunch of huge potato sacks that had been sewn together.

"You must be a friend of Gilbert's," I said as sweetly as possible. "I just want to know how you managed to get in here with nobody noticing. I only ask because I am pretty sure that any human that laid eyes on you would scream in horror. Plus, the moment that you reveal yourself to the non-Supernaturals, you are put on the Templar's hit list."

The supposed troll made a noise in its chest that I had to guess was a chuckle. Then it did something very interesting. It sunk into the floor. I mean completely submerged like it was dunking itself in a swimming pool. I swear I even saw a tiny ripple radiate out across the concrete.

"Hmm, that's new," I muttered, then I projected inwards. *Ladies, anytime you wanna speak up and give me a clue…*

That would be a granite troll, Betty spoke up. *Very nasty sort of creature.*

48

Okay, so how is it here, and what can I do to get rid of it? That seemed like a very logical set of questions.

I have no idea how it got here, but somebody obviously wants to do more than just kill a football player and have a better chance at winning a game. I believe this job was a setup to lure you out.

As Betty lectured me about the improbability of this granite troll and the possibility that I'd been duped, the concrete rippled and the teensy tiny head of the behemoth emerged like it was a periscope. As soon as it spied me, the rest of the body quickly emerged as well.

It made a series of sounds that might have had something to do with crushing me into a jelly-like substance and then using said jelly for a lubricant during self-pleasure. Or maybe he just made a bunch of random noises and I filled in what I thought he was trying to convey.

As it sorta waddled my direction, I did the only thing that I could think of...I let the switch-fingers go crazy. With one swipe, I raked the beast across its chest. Sparks flew and I think I saw a scratch in the surface, but other than that, I hadn't done anything resembling damage to it.

It swatted at me with a massive open hand, but it was as clumsy as it was huge and the swipe went over my head. I had no idea what to do. My only real weapons appeared ineffective. I was standing in the entry tunnel where I expected the team to arrive at any moment.

While the goblins had been invisible to the human eye, I was pretty sure that this troll would be seen quite clearly. This would not do at all.

I dodged a second swipe and then a flash of bright blue light flooded my vision. The troll seemed confused for just a second and it was then that I spied the large blade jutting from its chest.

Like an ocean wave, the troll rose up for a second and then crashed back down into the surface of the floor. This time I was certain that I saw the concrete ripple as the great creature melded into the floor leaving me alone in the corridor.

Almost.

"Let's get back to our seats before the team gets here," Race said nonchalantly. He was holding that big foam sword and shield I'd seen him waving about earlier.

"Please tell me you didn't kill that thing with a foam sword you bought from the concession stand," I said as we hurried up the tunnel and exited into the large service corridor just as a door slammed open and the team poured out.

"Glamour," Race replied with a shake of his head.

"Excuse me?"

"An enchantment. It hides the true appearance of the weapon. I have to be very careful, because it loses its magic anytime it is touched by anyone or anything other than me."

"And that sword just happened to be designed to kill a granite troll?" I was under the assumption that every Supernatural needs something special to kill or harm it.

"Any sort of iron will take down a troll," Race said as we made our way down the stairs that led to our front row seats.

"And you came to this game packing a weapon why exactly?"

"I knew that you were expecting trouble. I figured it would be prudent to carry something just in case you needed backup."

"I don't need protection," I snapped, flopping down in my seat and crossing my arms over my chest in a huff. I could almost feel another session of laundry looming in my future.

"No, you don't," Race agreed. "But it is always nice to know that somebody has your back. With Lisa away, I figured that person should be me."

I opened my mouth to argue, but nothing came out. I was about to have my butt handed to me by that troll and Race had dropped it like it was hot.

"I have no doubt that you can handle your business," Race said while my mouth continued to gape like a fish out of water. "But even the baddest of the bad can use a little support. I have no idea why, but the lines have been drawn and I choose to be on your side, Ava."

The crowd roared as the team erupted from the tunnel. I glanced up at the scoreboard. Two attempts on Colt during this game so far. Would there be more? And was that last one directed at him...or me?

That Ghoul Ava Sacks the Quarterback!

5

Get Lucky

The game could not get over fast enough. Race had rung my magic bell with his words of support. The fact that he was covering my back and not there to save me was the big winner.

The game was actually a bit dull as the second half dragged on. You could see the other team sort of give up, and our guys apparently did not feel the need to further demoralize and destroy them; not a mindset that I agree with, by the way.

I watched the last few seconds tick away and practically dislocated Race's arm yanking him from the seat and hauling him towards the exit. I don't know if you've been paying attention, but Ava need man!

We got to Race's van and since we were parked on a back street with very little lighting, I decided we were not going to make the one-hour drive home before I got what I have been so desperately craving. Also, Race and I seem to find things to argue about if we are forced into long periods of time with nothing to do but talk. (This might be the moment where some of you male readers skip ahead a few pages…I have been told that these sorts of scenes can make some of you squeamish.)

As usual, Race opened the door for me and I climbed in. The thing is, I slid right past my seat and into the back of the van. I was a little concerned about comfort. There certainly wasn't a bed or anything back here. My eyes fell on the large bench that ran down the length of one side. I hurried over and planted my behind on it to see what sort of maneuvering room might exist.

Directly above me was a weapons rack. Currently, it was empty. I gave it a very good yank to ensure that it was securely mounted. (Hee-hee…I said "mounted.") When it did not even wiggle slightly, I felt pretty sure that this was going to work. Just then, the driver's side door opened and Race climbed in.

"Ava?" Race called.

I saw his hand reaching for the curtain, so I decided to go for broke. I struck what I was hoping looked like an alluring pose. I'd slid to the far end of the bench so that I had one leg up on it and stretched out, the other sort of dangling down and curled back just a bit. My left arm was over my head and my right was reaching out for him.

All that was left was for me to say something to entice him to join me. I didn't know if I should go with funny or sexy or perhaps make an attempt at piecing together a clever double entendre. As per usual, all I came up with was Basic Ava.

"I can't wait any longer." I am so damn clever

Race stared at me and I started to hear the mother from *Carrie* screeching in my head. *They're all gonna laugh at you…*

I was just about to say something just as witty as my come-on line. Perhaps something like, "Just kidding." I'd laugh, he'd laugh, and we would pretend none of this ever happened.

Much faster than I realized he could move, Race Mitchell was through the blackout curtain and hunched over in front of me. Yeah…downside of this happening in a van.

He dropped to his knees and his hands came to my face. I'd seen those same hands wield a sword in battle, but in this moment, they were the gentlest things in the world. He traced the bottom of my jaw with his index finger and leaned in to me. Our lips touched and I could not help but gasp just a little. Seriously, that kiss went straight to my toes and then bounced back and swirled around the mommy regions.

I was actually afraid of the next part. I felt his tongue trace the entrance to my mouth and probe very gently. I opened up to him and had that split second of fear try to quell all the desire that had built up inside of me.

I really hate to break the mood here, but I know some of you might be so caught up in this that you have no idea what I am worrying about. Let me remind you about how I am technically dead. My body is not warm to the touch. Therefore, my mouth is absolutely nothing like yours—and that isn't even including the Sharkmouth aspect. I was terrified in that single second that the sensation would just be too much and this would end.

A strong hand slid down my side, lingered just under one breast for a moment, and then continued on towards the waist of my jeans. As his hand wandered, Race's tongue found mine and flicked it gently until my kiss met his with the same degree of passion.

It was only seconds later when I felt him pause. The moment that he did, my stomach tied up in a knot. Here it came. He was disgusted by me. The fact that I was not technically living would be the deal breaker. You might not think room temperature is a big deal, but when it comes to the human body, well, that just does not feel right.

"Ava," Race's voice came in a raspy whisper that, despite my knowing he was about to shut this down, gave me chills in my belly. I hadn't felt this way in as long as I could remember, and now I was going to have the rug yanked unceremoniously out from underneath me.

"Yes, Race?' I heard the whine in my voice that came from my longing and desire. It made me even more embarrassed.

"Once we cross this bridge, there is no going back. It will change things between us forever."

I was dumbstruck. That was not at all what I'd expected. I looked into his eyes and brought my hand to his face. He leaned into my touch and tilted his head down just enough to kiss the palm of my hand.

"I can handle it if you can." I gave him a smile and a wink.

He leaned into me and kissed me again. This time, his hands went to the waist of my jeans, traced them until he found the button, and then popped them open, easing the zipper down as he pulled. I lifted up as he slid them off me and then reached for his.

***

"Wow," I gasped as the two of us lay side-by-side, stretched out in the back of the van.

"Absolutely," Race agreed, his own voice still a bit breathy from exertion.

I have no idea how long our romantic interlude lasted. I did know that I'd accidentally ripped the blackout curtain down at some point.

"Well, at least we know one thing." I sat up and scooted so that my back was against the rear doors of the cargo bay.

"What's that?"

"Orgasms don't activate my switch-digits."

"Good thing." Race sat up and moved to be beside me.

We were staring out of the front of the van. There was a single streetlight just ahead and in front of where we'd parked; it was the only light, but it suddenly seemed incredibly bright. Maybe it was my vulnerability from being naked.

I was still thinking that when the light popped out and plunged the area into darkness. That was no big deal to me since I could see perfectly in the dark, but it was enough to put me on alert.

Maybe it was the throes of post-coital bliss, but for some reason, I had not heard or smelt the creatures that were now right outside the van. I rolled away from Race, and threw the sliding door on the side of the van open. Already my fingers and toes had gone switch and Sharkmouth was in effect.

I am not normally prone to running around naked; let's make that point perfectly clear. Despite having a brief stint as a stripper, I am still fairly modest when it comes to my body. That being said, I am more eager to not be killed…for good.

I saw something move away, and it took me just a few seconds to lock in on a pair of goblins. Both of them quickly realized that I'd spotted them and threw themselves down in the middle of the street. Each started pleading for mercy. This was very un-goblinlike behavior. At least in my experience, goblins are relatively fearless and have no issues with facing death. Yet, tonight I'd encountered some of the most craven examples of a goblin that could possibly exist.

"Please, Mistress Ghoul, we mean no harm," one of the dog-faced creatures yelped.

"What were you doing outside my van?" I snarled as I advanced. I was still looking everywhere for more trouble.

I could hear Race fumbling around as he apparently chose to at least put on his pants before exiting the vehicle. My enhanced senses told me that we were in the clear with the exception of a human that was just up the street and around the corner. Judging by the smell, he or she was not in the best of health. Considering the neighborhood, I guessed the individual to be homeless.

"We come with a message from Gilbert," the goblin replied. "We did not wish to interrupt your mating ritual and were simply waiting for you to be finished."

"Oh...okay." I guess that was a good enough reason. Then a thought struck me. "Were you the same goblins that I sent away earlier this evening?" I received vigorous nods. "And weren't there three of you?"

"Gilbert tore the head from Ear Pus and then beat us with the lifeless body as a punishment for our failure." The goblin who had so far remained silent looked up at me. One of its eyes was swollen totally shut and blood was leaking from the corner of its mouth.

"Let's hear the message." I accepted my clothes from Race who had climbed out of the van and was standing beside me.

"He says that he will gladly meet with you to discuss your terms. He believes that he can offer you something worthy in exchange for you allowing him to dispatch with the pathetic human, Colt Faber."

I was going to chalk up the use of the word 'pathetic' to the goblin making a direct quote. Looking down at the two, I doubted that they were in any condition to make disparaging remarks about anybody or anything.

At first I was ready to simply dismiss the offer. There was no way that I would be allowing Colt Faber's assassination. Then I came up with what I considered to be a brilliant if not simple plan.

"You tell old Gilby to meet me at my home tomorrow night and we will discuss a deal."

"Ava?" Race began, but as soon as I glanced his way, he put up his hands and shut his mouth in exaggerated fashion; going so far as to mime the whole lock-and-key thing.

The goblins scurried away, quickly vanishing into the darkness. I wondered very briefly if they had some sort of special means of travelling back to their master. After all, I did not see how else they could have returned to their master and then back to me in such a relatively short time.

What is your fascination with the goblin? Betty asked.

You say that like I am doing something wrong, I replied, making it a point to hopefully keep my face void of any notion that I was communicating with somebody inside my head. I know that Race is aware of my condition, but I just think these exchanges should be kept as low-key as possible.

Goblins are just not a very highly thought of species. As a human, it would be akin to you communicating with rats.

Never saw the movie Ben, *did ya?* I mused.

"What are you smiling at?" Race asked as I pushed my head through my shirt to find him standing directly in front of me. He had his eyebrows arched in curiosity.

"Just thinking about how long I had to wait for what we just did...and figuring out how I can convince you to make sure I don't wait that long again," I lied. It's only a little white lie. No harm, no foul.

"Well, since I am guessing you waited longer than just a day...I figure you gotta pretty good shot. I will be over tomorrow night." I opened my mouth, instantly thinking that he was already trying to pull some sort of knight-in-shining-armor crap in regards to my impending meeting with Gilbert, but he raised a hand. "Just give me a time. I can come before or after your little meeting."

"Race Mitchell, you are so getting lucky tomorrow night."

That Ghoul Ava Sacks the Quarterback!

Take On Me

"So you can basically focus on your master or whatever and somehow you get pulled to him in a flash," I essentially repeated what Nose Wart had explained.

"Well, there is no flash, Just Ava. It is simply a matter of the blink of an eye and we are before our master," Nose Wart said.

"Just a figure of speech." I gave a dismissive wave of my hand. "But the master can't send you someplace far away in the same manner." I rubbed my eyes. Betty and Blodwen were both tossing things at me and it was giving me a headache.

That most likely means Gilbert has some sort of witch or other Supernatural working with him, Blodwen was saying.

Unless they are utilizing a faerie Sidhe, Betty surmised. *That would be the only other way that these creatures are making it so deep into Morgan's territory before she is able to detect their presence.*

I heard the chimes announcing that I had a visitor. "Speaking of Morgan." I went to the front door and opened it to see the Psychic standing on my doorstep.

It was no secret that she was not pleased with my new residence. Betty had said that it had something to do with how the elves had woven in all the various sorts of magic security. Not to put too fine a point on it, but I guess my house was Morgan

61

proof. Something to do with elven magic. The residence actually existed only partially on this plane. That meant that Morgan could not detect me or any other Supernatural that was within the walls. Also, much like the faerie Sidhe, you could travel from specific locations called nodes and arrive within my residence.

I was actually a little baffled as to why one of Morgan's so-called friends would provide me with something so apparently powerful that obviously put Morgan at a disadvantage when it came to keeping tabs on me. I wondered that until the first visit from Queen Kari.

It had begun simple enough. The Dallas Psychic and elven queen had called me on my phone—I should have known something was fishy right then. She'd asked if I would give her permission to visit my residence so that she could see how well the crafters had done their job. Of course, I'd said yes.

I was in the middle of giving her a tour and telling her for the hundredth time that I was more than happy with my new digs when my chimes told me that I had another visitor. In considerable haste, Kari had excused herself to the location of the node where anybody I invite either arrives or departs.

When I'd answered the door, I had told Morgan that it was a pity; she'd just missed Kari. That had caused the normally unflappable Psychic to almost trip over my doorstep.

"Kari was here?" Morgan had asked.

"Just left, as a matter of fact," I'd replied.

"Can you show me where she arrived and departed from?"

It had seemed like a simple request. Perhaps Blodwen's gleeful chuckling should have been my first clue. When I'd showed the node to Morgan, the Psychic had whirled on me. For the first time ever, her facial expression actually reflected anger.

"I am going to dismiss this as your ignorance," Morgan had practically spat. Before I could object and try to refute her calling me ignorant, she had continued in an uncharacteristically stern tone. "I want you to promise me that you will notify me anytime somebody comes into your residence using that portal."

"You didn't know she was here," I'd gasped.

That had been the last time that I'd spoken directly with Kai. She hadn't ever requested to visit again. I still don't know if she and Morgan had ironed things out.

"I've been asked if a troll by the name of Gilbert may enter my territory," Morgan said by way of greeting.

"He's here to see me," I replied. If she wanted to be vague, then so could I.

"Also, I had a few pings on my radar." Morgan walked past me and headed to the large living room. I stood there like an idiot because she'd caught me off guard by using a slang phrase. Morgan was a proper sort and not one to "reduce herself" to the use of slang and the like. "Was that anything to do with you?"

"Nobody came through my node if that is what you are asking."

"And several of them blinked out in a short period of time."

"Yeah, that was me." So...she could sense when I killed the goblins the other night; or at least she could sense when they were no longer alive.

"And then a couple of them returned for a short period."

"Okay, I get it. Nothing goes on in your territory without you knowing." I threw my arms up in surrender. "An attempt was made on the life of a local football player."

"And was that rather large disturbance tied to this attempt as well?" Morgan smoothed her skirt underneath her as she took a seat on my couch.

"That would probably have been the granite troll," I replied as I sat down across from her. I thought I saw just the slightest twitch on Morgan's forehead. "That proved to be a bit of a challenge, but it was handled." She didn't need to know that it had been Race that put the big thing down. Hey, a girl has got to have a few secrets.

"So it seems that, despite my suggestions, you are going to continue to take outside work." Morgan leveled a gaze at me that would have probably had me babbling in seconds once upon a time; now, I just stared back. "You do realize that you are living in my district at my pleasure."

"Sounds good," I chuckled. "You could have claimed me a

long time ago. You chose not to, so that I would not draw any attention to you or some such thing. How's that working out for you by the way? Any news from the Council?"

From what I understand, there is some oversight committee that keeps the Psychics in check. It also seems that some of them may want Morgan out of the way. Just the rumor that she had a female ghoul in her district had been the Supernatural equivalent of a Third World country possessing a nuclear weapon.

"Don't be so glib." Morgan looked around the room. "Besides, I came with a reason. It seems that Lisa will be away for an extended period. I was to inform you so that you would not worry."

Now I knew she was screwing with me. For one, why would Lisa contact Morgan and not me. Also, not that it is a really big surprise, but how would Morgan know that Lisa is away in the first place?

"She is tending to some business for me in addition to the mission that she is running."

"And what mission is that?" I asked. I didn't care which one I got information about; either would be more information that I currently had.

"I don't ask her about her business, and as for what she is doing for me...I don't report my business to you, Ava."

You would be hard pressed to believe that I'd saved her life not too long ago. I'd even had to offer my services to the faeries before it was all said and done. Not all the faeries...just the godmother. That godmother, Rain, was currently living in an old Christmas tree forest on my other property. I'd sort of given her those woods as a gift. And, yay me, I had asked nothing in return.

"You're right," I agreed with a laugh that even sounded fake to me. "I was just curious. You know me...curious Ava the ghoul." Something was up and the silence inside my head was a very much in agreement with my sense of the situation.

"Have you seen Betty?" Morgan asked casually.

And there it is! I thought.

Tell her nothing, Betty insisted suddenly.

"Much like your business, Betty does not make me privy to hers. In fact, both of you are sort of closed off like that." I was kind of proud with how quick I came up with that response.

"She was going to check in with me when she was feeling better," Morgan said as she leaned back, her eyes never leaving mine.

Oh, why didn't I have my dark shades on right now? Solid black or not, I was worried that Morgan might see something in my eyes that gave away my lie.

"Wish I could help you," I said, doing my best to sound like I was not the cat who had eaten the canary.

"She sort of vanished off my radar as well. In fact, it was a lot like when that granite troll disappeared. There was a strong presence…and then nothing."

Don't listen to her, Ava, Betty warned. *She is trying to get you to make a mistake. She's laying a trap. You know she has no sense of anything inside your residence.*

"Again…really sorry that I can't help you. I'm sure she'll turn up. I've been kinda busy myself. You are welcome to wander around the house and see if you can find her," I said, struggling with keeping myself as free of emotion as possible.

Morgan made it look so easy. Hell, I knew a few ex-boyfriends that were just as adept at looking you right in the eyes and lying. They did not blink or bat an eye as they lied right to your face. I'd never been that good at it personally.

"Well, perhaps you can have her get in touch with me when she shows up."

"If she shows up, I'll definitely tell her that you are looking for her."

"If?" Morgan leaned forward, her hands clasped and her elbows resting on her knees. "Why would she not?"

Are you kidding me? She was going to nitpick me like that?

She knows, Betty sighed. *Maybe not the full story and the details, but she knows.*

So I tell her? I asked Betty.

Just as I opened my mouth, the answer came almost painfully. *No! You give her nothing solid. Having a suspicion is far from knowing the truth.*

"I will definitely tell her that you are looking for her," I said in a rush.

"Are you sure this is how you want to handle things?" Morgan sat back on the couch and crossed her arms, tilting her head just slightly to the side. "I thought that we'd gotten past this stage in our relationship. I believed that we'd reached a point where you could talk to me."

"I'm talking to you now."

"Yes, but you are being evasive, and you are acting like you are hiding something."

Worst poker face ever, I said to myself, not caring if I looked a bit crazier than normal. Of course, I already knew how bad I was at lying; having been told over and over by one boyfriend or another.

"I don't want to hear you giving anybody crap about being evasive," I snorted. "You have not been on the level with me since we first met."

"You are correct, Ava," Morgan replied coolly. "But I have my reasons. There are certain things that I did not, nor would I, share with you because of what you are."

I let that hang for a minute. I might not exactly like what Morgan had just said, but it was perhaps the most honest thing she'd said since the first day we met. The more I have learned about ghouls, the more I understand the reactions that I've received.

Seriously, get past the creatures that are terrified of me and look at how things have unfolded. I've had armies offered to me, a magical keep built by elves. More than one Psychic promising me the world in exchange for my service, and the Order of Templars developing special weapons in the hopes of just plain killing me despite the fact that I haven't really done anything.

If Morgan has knowledge on my abilities, maybe she is hoping that I won't learn or develop any more powers if she doesn't spill the proverbial beans. I could almost understand her logic…*if* that is the case.

I was about to suggest that maybe we open up a little to each

66

other. Maybe if we shared some information with each other, then perhaps we could bridge at least some of the gap between us. Unfortunately, (or fortunately—it remains to be seen) there was a chime signaling the arrival of Gilbert. Sure, it could've been somebody else, but I was pretty certain who it was that pounding on my door like they thought they could "accidentally" bust it in and claim that it was faulty workmanship.

"If you'll excuse me," I said to Morgan as I popped up and headed for my front door.

I was only a few steps away when I heard the scrabble of little clawed feet on my floor. A second later, a dozen goblins were sliding around the corner.

"There is a troll outside," Nose Wart snarled. "Nasty things and not to be trusted."

"Well, I need to speak with this one," I said as I reached the door.

"We will remain, Just Ava." Nose Wart barked something that I had to assume to be the goblin language and the entire group formed a line, each with his or her weapon drawn.

I have never seen such devotion in goblins before, Betty mused.

Maybe you just did not look close enough, I told her as I opened the door.

Standing in the doorway was a massive bulk of what could pretty much pass for human. He had all the human features, but up close, I could see patches of what looked like scales on his forearms. His face was almost pug-like and his buggy eyes rolled down at me to reveal dark brown irises that grew as his pupils reduced almost to pinpoints.

"So, you're the famous Ava Birch. Somehow I thought that you'd be bigger…tougher looking," Gilbert scoffed in a voice that was lower than the bass singer for the Oak Ridge Boys.

"Before we go any further, could you just say, 'giddyup-a-oom-papa-mow-mow' for me…just once." Those words came out before I had the chance to stop them.

"It is a wonder that you have survived this long," Morgan scolded as she stepped up beside me. "I am the regional Psychic, the one who gave you permission to be in this territory so that you could meet with Miss Birch."

The troll rolled his eyes over to fix on Morgan and his thin lips curled up in a very Grinchy smile. There was a degree of evil that rolled off this thing, and I was starting to struggle to keep my switch-fingers and toes in check.

It is said that trolls were spun from the essence of chaos, Betty said as I stepped back and held out my arm in a gesture of welcome. *They are perhaps the most unpredictable of creatures.*

"So, what is your real reason for doing all this?" I asked as the troll ambled in behind me like he didn't have a care in the world. And who knows…maybe he doesn't.

"What did that half-breed Anthony say?" Gilbert rumbled.

I spun around on the troll so fast that he was only a hairs' breadth from me when he managed to stop as well. I came up to about where I guessed his nipples to be and was staring at a chest that could double as a movie screen.

"We don't play it that way," I said. I caught the slightest raise of Morgan's eyebrows. I think I'd surprised her with my response. "I asked you a question. If you want to ask me one, then do it after you answer mine."

The troll scratched his head. "I thought you were be-ing…what's that word? Ret-something."

"Rhetorical?" Morgan offered. Good thing, because I wouldn't have come up with an answer nearly as fast.

"Sure." The troll shrugged again and then turned back to me. "The rumors say that you are kinda smart. I guess they were comparing you to something like a…" He faded and squinted his eyes in what I guess had to be concentration.

"A troll?" Morgan spoke again.

It took me a second for her comment to really register. "Hey!" I shot her a dirty look.

"So, why not illuminate her." Morgan didn't even look at me.

She doesn't know either, Betty gasped. *There is something going on and Morgan is just as in the dark as you are.*

"Seems sort of silly talking about this with a Psychic actually present," the troll grumbled.

"Humor me." Morgan gave a wave of her hands and turned as if she were walking away, but she only took a few steps.

"You want me to make you laugh?" Now the troll seemed beyond confused.

"It's just a figure of speech," I stage-whispered.

"Ohhh," the troll said. It took a few more seconds, but at last the elevator reached the top floor and he seemed to get it.

I've been watching a lot of horror movies this past year. Most of it was a form a research. Over time, I've come to actually enjoy some of the movies. One of the titles that has grown on me is the original 1978 version of *Dawn of the Dead*. There is a scene early on when the helicopter guy and the blond gal are at some terminal or something. A bunch of cops show up and it looks pretty bad for a minute. Then the two National Guards show up and things diffuse. Anyway, as everybody is going their separate ways, this one cop asks the intrepid heroes where they are going. The helicopter guy replies, "Straight up." This seems to confuse the policeman for a minute, and then you actually see a very dim light come on in his brain and he gets this doofy grin and starts nodding. That is basically the same sequence that played out on Gilbert's face.

Oh...and if you haven't seen the original *Dawn of the Dead*? You have my pity.

"You are on the soon-to-be-extinct list," Gilbert answered. "There is a bounty on your head so large that it is almost impossible not to take a shot. Sort of like when the humans' silly lottery ticket pool gets in the hundreds of millions. More people buy tickets, and lots of them are the type who don't normally buy them. It's almost funny to see how silly the humans get. At least it was until the price on your head came out." Gilbert nodded at me and then a smile creased his ugly face.

I knew that smile. He was about to do something stupid. I reacted just a second ahead of him and dove forward and under his massive hand that swished through the air where my head had been just a moment ago. Morgan apparently lacked the same degree of foresight. You'd think a Psychic would be dialed in a little better.

A series of yips sounded and my little goblin contingent charged the much bigger creature with that lack of fear to which I was accustomed. Of course they didn't fare very well. A single swipe of the other massive hand sent nine of the twelve careening across the room.

"Now you really did it," I snarled as I flew at Gilbert.

One of my hands found purchase in the shoulder and I drove the nails in as deep as I could. I hardly had enough time to celebrate my strike when I was slammed into a wall. To be more precise, Gilbert had driven himself backwards and pinned me between his body and the wall. My right arm was also caught, but both legs were still free.

I brought my knees up as much as possible and then kicked. The troll howled as both feet—the switch-toes to be precise— plunged into the beast's hamstrings.

I leapt clear as Gilbert slid to the floor. Blood was everywhere and I did not envy whomever it was that would have to clean up this mess.

By now, the goblins that had not been knocked senseless were charging, weapons drawn and ready to do some serious damage. I stepped forward and gave a shrill whistle.

"Everybody just wait," I barked. Kneeling down, I grabbed a handful of hair and jerked Gilbert's head up. "Who put the price on me?"

I was prepared for almost any answer. My money rested on the Templars; or at least the splinter faction of them that had been so active lately.

"You really don't know?" Gilbert chortled.

In one swift motion, I jerked his head back in a way that had to be painful, but that wasn't enough. In a flash, I punched him in the throat.

That sent the troll into a series of retching, hacking coughs. I hadn't done enough to totally crush his windpipe, but I'd hurt him. A little bit of blood frothed from his lips.

"Let's try that again," I hissed into his ear.

"Piss off, ghoul," came the strangled response.

"Why do we have to do this?" I asked the ceiling. I thought I saw a couple of the goblins look up as if to see who I might be talking to. "Perhaps I need to stop making threats."

"Good idea," the troll managed weakly as he continued to struggle drawing a full breath.

In a flash, I sliced off the left hand and popped it into my mouth like a piece of popcorn. A jet of blood sprayed my floor and Gilbert howled.

"I will ask once more…but only once." One of my switch-digits slid up the inside of his thigh and came to rest against one of man's more tender regions.

"The Psychics," Gilbert coughed.

That Ghoul Ava Sacks the Quarterback!

Fallen Angel

I sat in the corner licking my lips. Nose Wart waited patiently as I finished my meal. I could hear Gilbert as a whimper slipped past his lips. In my experience, bullies really are just a bunch of candy asses. One good punch in the mouth is usually enough to send them scurrying away in tears. In this case, I'd made Gilbert watch as I fed.

"Shut up, you big baby," I snarled.

"And you are certain about this order coming directly from the Council?" Morgan butted in again.

"You know, you can ask him that question another twenty or thirty times...I'm pretty sure that the answer isn't gonna change. How many ways do you want to hear him say yes?" I got up and allowed my meal to settle a bit.

Those first few seconds are kinda rough. I'd never actually seen myself in the mirror when I ate. One day, Lisa sorta insisted when I gave a her a bunch of crap for acting all squeamish about my feeding. Considering all she'd been witness to, I did not think that my feeding was any big deal.

I guess I never considered how my body reacted to consuming an entire adult human (or whatever might be on the menu). I settled in to eat like always and stopped after the first leg vanished down my throat. It was almost like watching a real life cartoon. I saw my body sort of swell up. My face got rounder and I looked like somebody had shoved a helium hose up my rear-end. I looked down at my clothes and expected to see the buttons straining, but all I did was just fill every little bit of my shirt and pants.

I briefly considered asking Morgan or Betty about it that day. Instead, I did an experiment. I stripped off my shirt the next time I ate. Sure enough, my entire upper body puffed out like a giant marshmallow. Next time, I ate without any pants. I would never do that again.

"For whatever reason, your body swells anywhere nothing is contacting the flesh," Betty had explained the next day. "If you were all bundled up with gloves, a scarf, hat and such, only your face would swell."

It only lasts a few seconds, if you blink, you would probably miss it. I wish things had been like that when I was alive. Imagine being able to eat an entire pint of ice cream and not have to increase your next session on the treadmill. Your body would just poof out once and then snap back into its regular shape.

Don't get me wrong, I am not talking about being skinny. Calista Flockhart can kiss my well rounded and properly curvy behind.

"I swear, mistress," Gilbert groveled, snapping me back to the scene at hand.

Ever since I'd held his manhood hostage, he'd been a blubbering sissy. According to Betty, he was acting according to the old ways when it came to dealing with a regional Psychic.

"When is the last time you heard from Losli?" I asked Morgan. I crossed the room to where Morgan sat at the large island in the center of my kitchen.

As I passed the troll, he recoiled as if I'd struck him. I stuck my tongue out and then climbed onto one of the tall barstool chairs. I was starting to feel a small gush of violent anger surging. At that moment, Betty and Blodwen both let out shrieks of surprise.

Ava, I need you to release Mystify again, Blodwen hollered.

Belay that, Betty barked a split second later. *I can handle*

74

this.

At first, it was like the onset of a headache. There was a dull ache right behind my eyes. It began to grow fast, and apparently it was so bad that I let out a groan of pain and dropped to my knees.

"Ava!" Morgan's face was inches from mine and she'd slapped me at least once as she tried to get my attention.

We could make this so much easier if you just submit your will to me, Ava, a familiar voice taunted me. *Let me out and I can show you what we are truly capable of. We can destroy the Templars once and for all, and put these Psychics in their place. Nobody would dare threaten us ever again.*

There is no us, Boudicca, I shot back. It was difficult to keep the comment inside my head. *And as soon as I figure out a way, you can bet I will be coming for you to put you down for good.*

The way is simple, you weak woman. Face me in combat. If you can defeat me, then I will cease to be. She paused and laughed, low and evil. *But* when *you lose, everything that you were and are shall cease to exist, and this vessel will be mine.*

Well, that is basically why I have not mindwalked since the discovery that Boudicca had somehow materialized in my head. I knew that I essentially absorbed the essence of any powerful Supernatural that I consumed, but I had no idea how or why the Patient Zero of female ghouls was now living inside me. As far as I knew, I hadn't consumed her.

"Ava, I need you to look at me," Morgan's voice drifted across the void that the pain in my head had created.

My eyes snapped open and I saw that I was now flat on my back. Morgan had my hand and she leaned in close to my ear and whispered, "You need to feed." She looked up and stared past me.

I let my head roll over to see what it was that she was looking at. It came as no surprise that I was looking at Gilbert. Fortunately for him, he was paying me no mind. For just a second, I had qualms about going over and eating this creature. For one, he looked mostly human.

"Screw it," I said.

Getting up, I walked over to the troll and raised one hand. I was ready to take his head off. That would be the easiest way to kill him as far as I knew. Then I would just lob off parts and chow down. For whatever reason, my little mental dust up with Boudicca had depleted me.

Worse still, I could sense Betty doing something inside my head. I was under the assumption that she was securing the warrior queen away in a secure space, but assumptions seldom work out for me. She'd asked me to free her up so that she could do what she needed to do.

I was still fuzzy on how that worked. It was not the first time that the request was made. Neither time had I really known what I was doing or what that meant. I think I would need to ask somebody very soon. Perhaps I could bounce the question off Morgan once everything settled down. Not that she was all that great at offering me anything useful in the realm of information, but she knew about Boudicca, and it is a safe bet that she does not wish for her to take me over.

I looked down at Gilbert, my hunger almost turning me inside out as it grew by the second. I absolutely needed to feed. This creep had come to my house and was set on killing me.

So why wasn't I just lopping his head off and putting his body to good use? I was just standing here, my arm pulled back, claws fully extended; but I wasn't following through.

If you ever saw that *Shrek* movie with Puss N' Boots, the one where Antonio Banderas did the voice, then maybe you recall when Puss got thrown outside. His eyes did that sad clown thing and he looked so darn cute. Well, Gilbert was sorta doing that now.

"Ah hell," I swore and stepped back, lowering my hand.

"Ava!" Morgan rushed over to me. "You need to feed now, and you will not be doing anything wrong by putting this cretin away once and for all, and allowing his worthless carcass to at least do some good in the world on its way out."

I almost sprained my neck jerking around so fast to look at Morgan. This was so unlike her. She was the calm in the storm.

She was never rash; or at least I'd never known her to be so.

"What gives?" I asked, taking a step back from the troll who was now beginning to sob. "And if you don't knock that off, I *will* eat you."

He sucked in his lower lip and took to just sort of shaking as he tried to hold in his crying. I had no idea that trolls were such sissies. However, I needed to put Morgan back in my crosshairs. She wasn't acting right and it had me concerned.

"If he is an agent of the Council, and they are seeking to take me down as well as kill you, then we need to adopt the philosophy of shoot first and ask questions later." Morgan was actually glaring at the troll!

"Who are you, and what have you done to my Morgan?" I asked.

It is truly Morgan, Blodwen spoke up inside my head. *And she has a point. Her anger is justified. This is unheard of...the Council does not send killers in to eliminate Psychics.*

"I need you to actually talk to me," I grabbed Morgan, but that sudden motion drove a spike of pain right between my eyes.

"And you need to feed...*now*," Morgan retorted. "I need you to be at full strength at all times, Ava Birch. I believe that both of our lives may...no...they *do* depend on it."

"Nose Wart!" I hollered.

"Yes, Just Ava," a voice said from right beside me. Hmm, I must've forgotten that the goblins were here.

"I need you to fetch—" I didn't even finish my statement. The little goblin was already racing off with three more of his comrades on his heels.

"Your mercy is misplaced," Morgan whispered. I was pretty sure she said it so low that only I could hear.

"Like I said, I need you to tell me what the hell is going on. For one, this is not like you. You are acting..." I let that statement trail off. I was almost frightened to express it out loud.

"We both have good reason to be afraid, Ava." Morgan was taking great care not to speak loud enough to be heard. She was basically just moving her lips, but my super hearing made her words crystal clear.

"Well then, maybe it is time for you to start talking. If this danger that has you so worked up includes me, then I think I have a right to know."

"You are correct," Morgan said after a long silence.

"Before I begin, I need you to promise me that you will stay silent until I finish. You have a way of interrupting and then sending a story off on a tangent that is almost impossible to return from."

I didn't agree with that assessment, but I nodded and promised to keep quiet until she was finished. As I did, Nose Wart arrived with not one, but a pair of bodies from my chiller.

I raised my hand even though Morgan had not yet begun. She nodded for me to go ahead.

"What about him?" I tilted my head over to where Gilbert the sissy troll was still planted on the floor and looking so pathetic that I had to wonder if all trolls were like this. Maybe they are all super sensitive or something. Although I hadn't picked up that vibe from Anthony.

"We either kill him or let him go. Just be aware that letting him go might spell disaster for us."

I thought it over. I just didn't want to kill the poor guy. The only problem remained in the fact that I wasn't too keen on being killed. This is that double-edged sword I keep hearing so much about.

Every single time I have had to commit an actual murder, I have foolishly told myself that it would be the last time. It does not seem that life is going to give me a break in that regard. I am a ghoul. Apparently, ghouls kill. I am told repeatedly about how fierce and scary they…we…are as a Supernatural. I am also told over and over that my biggest flaw is that I still think like a human. While I am not entirely ready to go all the way down the rabbit hole, it does look as if I will need to at least stick my head down and let the darkness seep into my being.

"Basement." I turned and walked away.

Never-ending Story

Gilbert's clothes were tossed in a corner. After I'd fed, I waited for a moment to see if he would show up in my head. Once I was fairly confident that wasn't going to happen, I settled in to hear Morgan's tale.

He was a common Supernatural, Betty explained. *You will actually absorb some of his strength, but a troll does not possess enough power to make the crossover.*

I would not point to the fact that Nose Wart's former mate, Butt Pimple, was in there with her. Granted, she was currently secured away in whatever dark box that Boudicca called home; but she was in there nonetheless. And she was a "mere" goblin.

"So, let's hear the story," I said as I leaned back against the wall and settled in.

"You remember Edward Losli?" Morgan began. I nodded.

He was some sort of Supreme muckity-muck on the Psychic Council. He'd been sort of flirty when we'd last met, and I think that was what finally pushed Race to make his move and ask me out.

"Yes, well he is dead." Morgan let that hang for a moment. "He was killed yesterday in his home. That means that those responsible were able to bypass his security."

"I did the same in Dallas," I reminded. "It might be hard,

but it isn't impossible."

"If he was just a regular Psychic, that would be true."

"So he is...was...some sort of super Psychic?"

"It is hard to explain, Ava." Morgan paused, and I was about to lay into her and demand that she just spit it out. It was time for her to stop being careful with what she told me. Then...she did exactly that.

"Edward was a necromancer. He was one of the individuals who came in and cleaned up after Adrianna's little mess. Many people credit him for saving the entire human race. Even the pope at the time acknowledged what he did and reportedly put in a sizeable sum to sweeten the final payment for services rendered. Breaking into his home would be on the list of perhaps one of the most impossible things to do...besides, we know who killed him."

I sat there and waited, but apparently Morgan wanted to draw this out. As I stared at her, I started to rethink my assumption for her not telling me. If I didn't know any better, I would swear that—

"His name is Andrew Losli...Edward's brother. He was my...lieutenant until he disappeared. After a search was made, I had him declared dead."

Morgan turned away from me and now I was certain of at least one thing; Andrew Losli was more than just Morgan's lieutenant. Still, I would wait for her to spill the truth. If I had to ask, then I would always wonder how much she left out. It's not like she probably wouldn't still withhold information, but if I didn't ask questions, she might just get into a rhythm and say more than if I interrupted.

"We were lovers for almost a century."

And there it was. The other shoe had just metaphorically dropped.

"He is perhaps the only person that would be able to get into Edward's home. Witnesses say that he simply knocked and Edward threw the door open to his long lost brother. Once inside, it is unlikely that Edward even knew what his brother was doing until it was too late. His magic was...powerful." Morgan turned back to face me and I saw a look in her eyes that made me pretty sure she was having a hard time telling me this. At first, I didn't know why.

She will have a difficult time upholding that image of powerful perfection that she has cultivated, Betty offered. *This is a piece of her humanity, and somebody like Morgan does not show that aspect...to anybody.*

Especially if that anybody is me, I quipped.

"I tried to dismiss the coincidences. So much activity in my district the past several months." She turned to me and I saw something in her eyes that I could not figure out; then she said the words. "I am so sorry, Ava. All this time, I have tried to dismiss this as your fault. The appearance of a female ghoul in my district was an easy choice to place the fault and the blame. I did not want to believe that it could be Andrew. There had always been a bit of a zealot that seeped through his personality. He spoke often of the old days when the Supernaturals were divided between the undead and all the others."

"I don't understand," I blurted. "Aren't all of you...us...aren't we all sort of under the same heading when it comes to the non-human thing?"

"There was a separation that happened long ago." Morgan paused. "When Boudicca came to power, the undead members of the community turned to her and exalted her. They called her their queen and believed that she would lead them into battle against humanity. Humans would become slaves and feeding stock."

I let that sink in for just a moment. Why would the undead Supernaturals want that? A flash came from deep in my mind and Boudicca gave me the answer. I could feel it pouring from her in waves.

"The undead were considered lesser beings in the Supernatural community," I whispered.

"I am ashamed to admit it...but yes," Morgan said in a voice that was barely audible. "It seems that no society is free from prejudice. Perhaps it is simply a construct of the conscious mind that insists there must be a better and a lesser. And of course...don't we all want to be the better."

"How many types of undead are there?" I asked out of honest curiosity.

Morgan looked up at me and cocked her head to the side. She studied me with very close to her usual lack of expression for several seconds, then, she smiled. She actually made a sound that was very close to a laugh.

"And there is that human side of you again."

"What do you mean?"

"You are trying to quantify something that has no set number. It would be the same as asking how many types of humans there are on this planet."

"But humans are just humans," I sputtered.

"And the undead are just the undead," Morgan said flatly. "They were once living, and then they died. For some reason that nobody can understand or explain, they have returned. Nobody can say how or why.

"When some of the first vampires appeared, the Vatican demanded they be brought in for a full inquisition. None of the vampires survived, but the rumor is that they were asked about what waits for us beyond this physical world. The scrolls say that not a single one of them could recall anything from their time being dead. It is believed that this is where the division began. The conclusion was drawn that the vampires must have been denied access to Heaven. That meant they were evil...damned. Since then, other cognizant undead have suffered the same sort of inquisition. Not one has been able to say what lies beyond. It is for that reason that the undead were seen and have been labeled as being evil beings condemned to Hell."

"And so it is assumed or decided that we are all soulless?" I snapped.

I'd heard that word thrown at me before. I'd met those who felt as this Andrew Losli person apparently feels. Now I wasn't so sure that this assumption was correct. Who were they to say that I'd lost my soul?

"...to be sure. Only, it is simply not possible to confirm the theory either way." Morgan's voice brought me back to the situation at hand. I hadn't spaced out that completely in a while.

"Can we go back to the part where you were dating this creep?" I asked, doing my best not to sound snotty. I didn't want to say anything that might shut Morgan down.

"Andrew is…was a lovely man," Morgan began. I could tell that this was difficult for her. There was a strain to her voice that was very foreign sounding coming from her. "Shortly after the turn of the century, he did something that we are forbidden to do. He sought out his family."

"Sort of how you went back to your village after they told you not to?" I probably shouldn't have asked that. but sometimes my big mouth just shoots out stuff.

"No, not anything at all like that," Morgan shot back tersely. "For one, I did it shortly after my training, he did it centuries after he'd become a Psychic."

"Why? None of those people would know him?"

"Apparently he had been keeping tabs on his human family for hundreds of years. He was fascinated by them, much like people are with pets. Also, apparently he was watching for any signs that another member of his family might be gifted in some way. None of us had any idea that he was waiting for one thing specifically." Morgan paused, maybe for dramatic effect, but I was leaning forward now, so it worked. "Andrew and Edward were twins. Andrew was waiting for another set to be born. According to what was discovered in a journal of his that I found shortly after he vanished, he believed that twins would be the most likely to possess the same spark that he and Edward possessed."

"And so he found out about twins, and that is what set him off his rocker?"

"No. Andrew stayed very close, but he did not make an attempt to contact them directly. He blames himself for the fact that he maintained that distance and believes that they would have been saved if he'd been there the night they were attacked by a vampire."

And there it was. It's always something like that, isn't it? One person has a bad experience with something and then anything remotely related gets painted with the same brush. Seriously, think about it. It happens all the time.

"The thing is, I should've known better," Morgan whispered. "I was blinded by my love for Andrew, and so when some of the undead Supernaturals in this community began to vanish, I would look into it, and when I could not find the answer, I wrote it off to perhaps a vamp that let the time slip away, or perhaps a ghost that simply chose to move on."

"So you are saying that he was preparing for this right under your nose and now you feel responsible."

"Worse." Morgan's voice was practically inaudible again.

I knew that I wasn't going to like this. Maybe I would get lucky and she would suddenly revert back to that Morgan who told me next to nothing. Still, after I waited several seconds and she had not said anything, I needed to at least try and prompt her.

"How can it be worse?"

"I helped him."

Desperate but not Serious

Did you know all this? I asked Betty.

This is Morgan we are talking about, child, the woman sniffed.

Morgan had left about ten minutes ago. I was still reeling. Some of what she had revealed was not that big of a deal, but the fact that she'd revealed to this Andrew Losli a number of very secret and close guarded methods of eliminating members of the undead Supernatural community was cause for concern.

It didn't matter that she'd named him her lieutenant and he'd convinced her that the threats to her life were real, she'd divulged this information without approval from the Council. By doing so, she'd given a zealot the means to eradicate those creatures that he'd deemed abhorrent.

Yeah, but her doing something like this is so un-Morgan-like, I said as I sighed inwardly.

I think it is time that you start accepting the fact that the Supernatural world is just as flawed as its human counterpart. More so actually, Blodwen added, making her presence known for the first time in quite a while. *We have had much more practice at being deceitful, cruel, and just plain deceptive. Our existence has relied on that last one for hundreds if not thousands of years.*

I was thinking of a reply to that statement when there was a knock at my door. I wasn't expecting anybody. My built-in security hadn't done anything, so I had to guess that it was somebody (or something) that was basically harmless.

I turned the knob and was surprised to see Kayleeni standing on my doorstep. My surprise was quickly replaced by shock and concern. She was covered in blood and her left eye was swollen shut. Her golden skin was a mottled brown and before I could really register what was happening, she said, "They grabbed Anthony." After that last word escaped her lips, she fainted.

I knelt down and was glad to see that her chest was rising and falling. Scooping her in my arms, I carried her inside and yelled for Nose Wart. He arrived in a flash with a dozen goblins on his heels.

As they all stood staring at me and then sneaking peeks at the unconscious water elf, I was listening to Betty and Blodwen rattle off a list of what I would need to help this poor thing. Now that I had her on my couch, I could see that whatever had gotten ahold of her had done quite a number. Her left arm had an extra bend between the wrist and elbow that was definitely not there the last time I saw her.

"Okay, here is what I need," I barked as soon as Betty gave me the last ingredients.

In minutes, I had a huge iron cauldron filled with warm water and a box of sea salt. In addition, there were a variety of flowers and what I would have mistook for weeds; but apparently goblins know their herbs and had grabbed exactly what I required.

"I didn't know that we had chamomile growing in the back yard," I mused as I crushed it and added it to the water.

"A very complete garden has been planted and put into place for you, Just Ava." Nose Wart looked up at me with a smile. "When Aoife returns, she will be quite pleased at some of the rarest herbs that the elves put in the greenhouse."

I almost felt bad that I'd not thought of the siren in a while. She'd been gone for months now, and I had no idea when she might return...if ever. Apparently Nose Wart was not of the same mind.

I scooped up Kayleeni as I was told and then laid her down in the cauldron. I had a moment of human weakness or whatever you want to call it as she slid beneath the surface of the water. I watched and waited for her to react. If she looked to be in distress, I was going to snatch her from the water in a real big hurry.

I was standing there next to the cauldron just waiting when my security system made a bit of noise. A moment later, a pleasant female voice informed me, "Intruder approaching from the east."

"Umm...which way is that?" I asked the air, not expecting an answer.

"Turn to your right," the voice prompted.

"Whoa...cool," I breathed, and then I turned right and headed for the window. It was just about midnight, so I had to discount the likelihood of it being a human.

There was a scrabbling of feet behind me and I turned to see the goblins rushing to keep up as they all drew their assorted weapons. Nose Wart was the only one not pulling his sword, instead, he was more concerned with catching up to me.

"Shall I sound for the jötunn, Just Ava?" the goblin asked as he fell into step beside me.

"No sense in getting them all riled up if it's nothing," I answered with a wave.

Just as I reached the window and opened it, a voice bellowed from outside, "Ava Birch, I am here to put an end to you. Come out now and face me in combat."

I looked outside and saw a troll that resembled Gilbert in the middle of my rose garden. Huh...I have a rose garden. Learn something new every day.

"And who might you be?" I called out after opening my window.

"I am Goran Magma, brother to Gilbert. I felt his departure and know that he was here with you. I can only assume that you killed him." Three more massive trolls stepped forward to join

Goran.

"No need to assume. I did it." I glanced down at Nose Wart and whispered, "Perhaps you can go ahead and send for the jötunn."

Nose Wart nodded and took off at a sprint. As soon as he did, another goblin took his place. It was a female.

"I shall remain at your side until my sire returns, Just Ava," Teat Mucous barked (at least that was my guess as to who this could possibly be).

"You say you felt his departure?" I challenged. "So are you some sort of Psychic...or is this a power all trolls possess?"

I was actually just firing blanks. I had no real idea what a troll may or may not be capable of; yet there was something strange in how he'd said that bit about feeling his brother depart. It was, for lack of a better way to describe it, like a bad high school play. The line was too rehearsed and there was just a bit too much emphasis on the way he claimed to have 'felt' something.

Very good catch, Ava, Betty praised. *I have dealt with trolls on many occasions and have not known a single one that could do such a thing.*

"You get to ask no questions, Ava Birch," Goran retorted. "You simply get to choose whether to die quickly or slow. I am hoping that you choose slow. There is much I would like to do to you before allowing you the peace of a final death."

"Then this is your lucky day, big fella," I shot back. "I'm going for the resist and fight thing. So I guess that means slow. Just be aware that I doubt you have what it takes. Oh, and when I kill you and devour you, at least then you will be reunited with your brother."

That seemed to be the magic phrase, because the troll charged toward my keep. Personally, I had no idea what he believed he would accomplish by attacking my house, but to each his own. I was also not sure what all of the security features of my new home had up its sleeve. It didn't take long to find out.

At some point during that charge across my lawn, Goran had either been passed or—and this was more likely—he al-

88

lowed one of his henchmen to get ahead just in case there might be some sort of lethal security. There was a crackle that reminded me of water being dripped onto a hot frying pan full of oil. I saw a flash of red that seemed to be like a force field wall. Funny, because I'd known for a fact that the goblins, bugbears, and even the jötunn frequented that area. Not one of them had ever triggered a red force field wall. Did I mention that it vaporized the troll that collided with it?

Goran and the rest of his little band of raiders pulled up short. One of them skidded a bit too far and just barely made contact with the red wall of death energy. I guess it didn't matter the degree of force in the collision because he went up in a cloud of black ash as well.

"So, you are a coward!" Goran raged, stalking back and forth a good few yards away from where the force field waited.

I wish I could freeze the image on his face when I stepped out my front door and walked around the side of my house. I stalked across the yard and stopped about ten yards from the irate troll.

"Actually, I am more than willing to fight you one on one," I said calmly.

Of course, the voices of Betty and Blodwen had erupted when I'd started for the door. That is why I locked them away. I didn't need the distractions. Believe it or not, fighting takes a considerable amount of concentration; at least it does if you plan on staying alive.

"Those are brave words from the other side of that force wall," Goran scoffed.

"Says the troll with a small army backing him up," I shot back. "Oh…wait. Down to just one? Sucks to be you."

Honestly, I had no idea where this bravado and crap comes from. I will admit that I have become a fairly proficient fighter. It helps when you don't actually feel pain. I wondered if Goran knew about the ghoul's ability to completely block out pain.

The troll made a gesture with one hand and his lone remaining minion backed away. He stopped at the trees that lined that side of my property. It looked to be about the same distance as I was from my house. I guess that was fair.

I started towards the troll and only winced a little as I passed the twin piles of fine ash that marked where both trolls had been disintegrated. Once I was sure I was clear, I stopped approaching and willed my switch-digits to extend.

"Here I am."

I threw my arms out wide and let my fingers wiggle a bit. My eyes scanned the area and I was actually surprised that there were no other beasties hiding anyplace—or at least none that I could detect.

Goran seemed to do the same thing. I don't think he believed I was brave or crazy enough to actually come out and face him in battle. To quote my favorite animated rabbit, "He don't know me very well...do he?"

The quiet of night suddenly seemed deafening as we faced each other across the open field. It was as if I could hear the individual blades of grass rubbing against each other. I moved to my right and he did likewise. We circled each other this way until I was now close to where his follower could reach me if he charged and perhaps caught me off guard.

I stared into Goran's eyes and did not like what I saw looking back at me. There was a degree of fear—which I didn't mind—as well as a lot of hatred. I realized that I'd killed his brother. I guess it didn't matter that his brother had started it.

When he charged, I simply crouched and waited for him to get close. This tactic had been the same that I'd used against a few of my larger opponents. I was all ready for him to over-commit and then I would side-step and slash.

I found myself tumbling end over end and slamming into the base of a massive tree. Somehow, Goran had stopped on a dime and waited for my slash. After I missed terribly, he back-handed me and sent me flying.

"That didn't go at all how I planned," I grumbled as I stood up.

My body tipped over and I found myself sprawled on my stomach as the troll came stomping my direction. I looked down to see my right leg sitting at a funny angle below the knee that I was pretty certain was not natural.

I was trying to get up when he reached me and reared back with one massive leg and punted me. He was smarter than I gave him credit; he kicked me so that I flew even further from my home. I was struggling to my knees and trying to figure out a way to defend myself from another attack when the distinct sound of a gun being fired boomed just to my right.

"What did you do with Anthony!" the voice demanded.

I turned and was surprised to see Colt Faber standing just on the edge of the clearing near my driveway. He had a pretty nasty looking pistol pointed at Goran. He was smart enough to place himself in a position where he could cover the lone remaining miscreant that had come with the pissed off troll.

"This is a bad idea, Colt," I called. "You don't know what you are messing with."

"I know enough," the man retorted, not taking his eyes off of his target and the troll just past him still standing near the trees where he'd retreated to just before this debacle began.

"Actually…I don't think that you do."

Talking to Colt was not enough of a distraction to block out the pain. I started rolling a song by Wakko from the *Animaniacs* in my head. It is the one where he lists all the capitals of the United States.

I climbed to my feet. Colt glanced my way and staggered back a step before recovering his composure. It looked like he was going to be sick. I guess my leg looked worse than I thought. I certainly wasn't going to look down at it.

…and here is Providence, Rhode Island next to Dover, Delaware…

"Stupid human, you just made my night easier." Goran took a step forward and Colt pulled the trigger.

I was actually impressed. Most times, when you see one of those corny movie standoffs, the bad guy basically walks up and takes the gun from the good guy (or gal) and then either kills them or gets away. Apparently Colt was not afraid to shoot. Unfortunately, the bullet seemed to have about as much of an effect on Goran as a spit wad.

The angry troll closed the distance between himself and Colt in three steps. I had to act or the stupid human was going to end up dead. Any chance our team had of winning the championship would die in my yard, and I couldn't have that, now could I.

With a single bound—yeah, I was surprised that I could jump on this leg too—I landed on the troll's shoulders. I plunged one set of switch-fingers into his neck and then heaved back. I landed on my butt with a dull thud and winced as the massive troll continued to advance on Colt.

It took one more step and then paused. I looked down in my lap and saw a large ugly face staring up at me. Its mouth was still moving, and the expression was a nasty sneer. Then, the eyes went dull and the body toppled with a loud thud that was punctuated by a gout of blood shooting from the neck stump.

I didn't waste any time, nor did I consider Colt's sensibilities. I popped that huge head in my mouth like it was a giant gumball. With a few serious chomps, I was already starting to feel better. I could also feel my leg knitting itself back together. I stood up just as another sound caught my attention.

Colt had fainted.

"I told you that you didn't know what you were messing with." I sort of limped over to him and looked down at the unconscious human.

"Actually, he knows quite a bit," a voice said from beside me, causing me to jump.

I pulled up just in time to prevent my switch-fingers from decapitating Kayleeni. Truthfully, I probably would have missed. I think my swipe would have gone right over her head.

"Don't ever do that," I scolded.

"Sorry, I asked where you were and one of the goblins explained that you were out here preparing to meet Goran in single combat," the water elf said, hardly giving my claws a second glance.

"This isn't over yet, ghoul!" Goran's minion shouted as he turned and ran off.

"You're right," I called to the sky, not knowing or caring who heard me. "I still got me a troll to eat."

"Cool," Kayleeni gasped as I sliced off a leg and started to chow down.

When I was finished, the two of us walked back to the house; I had the still-unconscious Colt slung over my shoulder like a sack of flour. I watched with mild curiosity as the water elf strolled past the two piles of ash. If I was correct, the force field only took out people who were unwelcome or meant me harm. I was guessing that it was more to do with the latter. If it took out every unwelcome visitor, I would decimate the door-to-door religious folks, home siding salesmen, and Morgan.

That Ghoul Ava Sacks the Quarterback!

10

More than a Feeling

"So, who took Anthony?" I asked as Kayleeni and I walked into my entry hall. I was seeing way too much of this part of my house lately.

"I thought that it was Goran and his people, but now I'm not so sure." The water elf's eyes began to brim with tears. "There is a rumor, but if it is true, then this is far more serious than a football player."

"Yeah…well I would go with the assumption of it being bigger than just Colt." I was debating on how much to tell the water elf when I spotted a familiar figure standing under the arch made by my wrap-around staircase.

Morgan was waiting for me just inside. She shot a glance at the form I carried with me. I could tell that she had some serious misgivings about a human coming into this situation, but there wasn't much I could do about it at the moment. I certainly wasn't going to just leave him outside.

"I believe I may know who is behind this," Morgan stated. "If I am correct, then you might find yourself tested unlike ever before."

"That is always encouraging." I made sure that Colt was comfortable and covered up on one of those benches in my entry hall. Until this very moment, I'd not actually seen a use for those things. Seriously, who sits around in an entry hall?

I walked into my actual living room and flopped down on my favorite recliner. This was one of those times that I hated the fact that I did not need sleep. A good nap would have been super sweet.

"And just how much information are you going to share with me on this little operation?" I asked, not caring that I sounded sort of bratty at the moment.

"This is not some regular mission, Ava." Morgan was her calm and cool self. I both hated and envied that ability of hers. "I do believe that what we are facing is the opening salvo of the actual war."

"I keep hearing about this war, but I am still more than just a little bit fuzzy about the particulars. I mean, I get the part about how the Templars want to finish the job that they started when it comes to wiping out the ghouls…at least the female version. What I am not so sure about is what else remains after I am wiped out."

"You haven't told her?" Kayleeni gasped. "She doesn't know that it is her potential to expose our entire society to the humans?"

"Not entirely, *thank you* very much," Morgan snapped. "And I will have you know that I have been acquainted with Ava since shortly after her inception. You have not known her for more than a few hours. Do not presume to tell me what she should and should not know. She needs to have this dosed to her in manageable bits. If you heap too much on her, she may well buckle under the weight."

"Ummm…standing right here," I sniffed.

Morgan is correct, Ava, Betty spoke up. *She has warred with you being told about certain aspects. Part of it is due to your refusal to stop seeing our world through human eyes. There is much that separates us from them.*

"When we have tried to tell you about bringing our sort into the light, you have dismissed the notion." Morgan turned to me. "And while there are many who dismiss the old prophecies, I have seen too many of them come to pass."

"And do the Templars know about these prophecies?" I asked.

"They do," Morgan answered calmly. "And it is perhaps that reason why they are so intent on your destruction."

"Why?" That didn't exactly make sense to me.

"If you do as the prophecies state, then they will no longer be necessary." Morgan paused, and I knew there was more. At last, she continued, "And some of them fear that may cause their magic to become inert. There is word that they have been gifted their agelessness until their mission is complete."

"But wouldn't killing me do the same thing?"

"No. The belief is that we have been kept alive this long because of the possibility of your return." Race stood in my open front door. My senses must really be on the fritz if somebody was able to open my door without me knowing. "If you are struck down, the faction that is clinging to that old belief feels that they will be kept alive to defend against the *possibility* of another such as yourself that may arise in the future."

"You realize how silly all this sounds?" I snarked. I walked over to Race and planted my hands on my hips. "And what do you believe? Because if you think that my death would mean the end of your existence, then it makes sense as to why you have decided to take my side. That would also mean—"

"Enough, Ava," Race said with force, but without raising his voice. "If I was only here keeping you alive out of such a selfish reason, then last night would not have happened."

"Wait, what happened last night?" Kayleeni popped up in between us. She looked first at me, then Race. Her mouth made a tiny 'O' as she figured it out. "You two? Really?"

"You can't be serious?" Morgan uttered, shaking her head in disbelief.

I spun on her, and in the blink of an eye, had crossed the room to be right in her face. "Before you go jumping on whatever moral high horse you think you can ride around on, who I have relations with is none of your concern."

Morgan took a step back and brushed her hands down her blouse as if my proximity had gotten her dirty or something.

That only pissed me off more.

"I am doing no such thing. I apologize if it seemed that way."

I might have actually staggered backwards a step. Unless I'd just gone mental, Morgan had just apologized to me. Me! Twice in one day!

"Ava, you need to understand that I have only kept your best interests in the foremost of everything that I have done. Whether it was the decision to tell you something, or *not* tell you."

"Wait, so how did you think not telling me about some of the things I have faced could be a good thing? I seem to recall a vampire who invaded the area…" Of course that was simply one instance of several, but I think she saw where I was headed.

"A ghoul is not something to be trifled with," Morgan replied. "However, I had my doubts about you. All the way up until that day you drew me into the heart of the Sidhe to save my life, I did not believe you to possess the traits nor the ability to act as a ghoul. If I am being truthful, I still have my doubts."

"You aren't doing a very good job of winning me over, Morgan," I snarled. How had she gone so fast from apologizing to basically kicking me in the teeth?

"I am not seeking to win you over. The real truth in the matter is that I worry about your humanity."

There it was again. Over and over I'd been accused of thinking too much like a human. I had no idea what else I was supposed to think like.

"Ava, a ghoul is a killer. That is their purest essence. When they are in battle, that is when they truly shine and the best of their abilities can be seen. Just a short time ago, you did not wish to take the life of a troll that had been sent to kill you. A true ghoul would have simply struck, fed, and moved on."

"Yeah? Well maybe this human side of me is exactly what I need. Perhaps that is the trait that I possess that no other ghoul before me has, and just maybe that is what will allow me to bring the Supernatural community into the public…or the light if that is the word that makes you all feel better."

Morgan opened her mouth, but just as quickly shut it. Race moved around and looked at me, his arms folded across his chest. Even the water elf had stepped back and was now regarding me with something in her expression that had not been there just a moment ago.

"Dear lord," Morgan gasped.

I believe you just hit the nail on the head, so to speak, Betty piped up. *I don't believe that any of us considered that possibility before.*

"She may just very well be onto something." Race clasped his hands behind his back and began to study me with a look that I did not like on somebody who was supposed to be my lover.

Almost as if he could read my thoughts, he shook his head and cleared the expression from his face. He turned to Morgan. "Has nobody ever considered the fact that Ava is so different from the stories? Perhaps that is exactly how she will do what it is that so many fear she has been sent to do."

"I can certainly say that the thought never crossed *my* mind." Morgan stepped closer to me and put her hands on my shoulders. I thought she was about to say something deep and meaningful; or maybe she would even apologize again. "Perhaps it will be okay for you to cling to that last vestige of your human nature a while longer."

Okay, so not an apology or anything of that nature, but perhaps she'd used her quota for the decade. I gave a nod that let her know I was good with things.

"This is so cool," Kayleeni breathed.

Everybody turned to look at her. If that had been me getting so much attention at once, I might've blushed or simply taken a step back. Kayleeni did no such thing. She had this expression like a child seeing the present of their heart's desire under the tree on Christmas morning. At least she did for a few seconds. Suddenly her expression fell.

"What is it?" I asked. Curious as to what had just popped her bubble.

"Anthony."

That single word snapped me back. In all the madness, I'd

simply forgotten that her arrival had been to tell me that something had grabbed the half-troll. Then another thought came: Morgan had said that she thought she knew what might be behind all this. I was hoping the two would be the same.

"Keyoggia." Morgan stepped up beside me. At first I thought she was saying something to me in some odd language. Then I saw Kayleeni nod vigorously. "Are you certain?" the Psychic asked the water elf.

"I only caught a glimpse as he appeared. His arrival came with enough force to send me across the room and slam me into the wall. I think I lost consciousness," Kayleeni explained.

"That would be not only unprecedented...but very bad," Race spoke, sounding more than just a little concerned.

"Excuse me?" I raised my hand and stepped into the triangle created by the three. "What is a Kellogg-gee-ah?"

"Keyoggia," Morgan corrected. I hadn't even been close in my pronunciation. "He is ogre magi."

"I think I saw one of those in that Dungeons and Dragons monster book," I said excitedly.

That book had actually been Betty's idea. She told me that many of the monsters contained in that game were based on real Supernaturals. There was a big conspiracy in the Supernatural community as to who had leaked the information. Apparently it is like that massive Grimoire that can only be purchased on Amazon.su for a few million bucks. Perhaps I should amend that statement in that it is a very dumbed down version of the Grimoire.

"That would explain some of the recent events," Morgan said, almost sounding like she was talking to herself. "Goblins being teleported into my district, along with that granite troll. And now, simply popping in and abducting one of my denizens."

That was the first time I'd heard Morgan make any sort of connection between herself and the Supernaturals in her district. It seemed to me that she was building a head of steam.

"And now I am certain who is behind this and helping the Council." She turned to me and I saw true anger blazing in her eyes. "I was a fool, Ava. I should have seen the writing on the wall and gone ahead and claimed you. I just hoped that by leaving you free, such as it is, that perhaps the others would not see me or this district as a threat. I guess I simply forgot what sort of power a female ghoul means."

"Do it, I want to be able to say that I was here." Kayleeni had popped up between Morgan and I again, and her gaze kept shifting back and forth between us. She was actually bouncing up and down on her toes.

"Umm, what am I missing?" Yeah, that's me, always the last to the party.

"What would you say if I asked you to be claimed by me and my district?" Morgan asked.

I was actually struck speechless. I had become used to the fact that I had no ties. Not that I really knew what that entailed.

This is probably for the best, Betty piped up.

I was pretty sure that I was broadcasting everything inside my head since she was obviously following along with the conversation.

I do believe that it will be the two of you standing together for the foreseeable future, Blodwen weighed in. *Perhaps this is the best option.*

"Before I agree to anything, I want to know what this means. What will it change? Am I going to be some sort of servant or subject who has to do whatever you say?" I challenged.

"It is nothing like that at all. If I claim you for my district, then it will simply allow me to always sense where you are...although I don't know if this house will prevent my sensing you the way it has with other Supernaturals. It will also allow you to know where I am."

That last part was interesting. I never knew where Morgan was at any given moment. Still, it seemed strange and a bit simple. Being bonded to her sounded so formal and official.

"There is one other gift that will come from this." Morgan glanced down at Kayleeni as if she expected the water elf to beat her to the punch and divulge whatever it was that she had not revealed. "You will have a sense of all your fellow members of

101

this community. Supposedly this is a trait that only ghouls possess. It apparently made it so that the ghouls could be dispatched to deal with anybody that got out of line or sought to usurp or turn on the regional Psychic."

I was feeling myself struggle with something that was obviously more than I probably understood. After all, I'd been offered castles and even armies. Morgan wasn't offering anything.

"Is this permanent?" I asked, suddenly curious as to the depth of this bonding or claiming or whatever it was supposed to be.

"For as long as I am alive. Unlike most of the other Supernaturals, my passing would not transfer you to my successor. In fact..." Morgan paused and some sort of realization seemed to strike her. "That is the case with all of the undead Supernaturals."

"But I can't...like, just say I want out once I have agreed?"

"No, Ava. If you do this, it will bind us permanently."

Despite the renewed and almost urgent prodding of both Betty and Blodwen, I still hesitated. This was a bigger step than marriage from what I gathered. And marriage hadn't really worked out that well for me. To go into this with the knowledge that I was stuck? It just sounded really scary.

"So why aren't you offering me something like an army or obscene wealth or some such thing? You are basically asking me to do this for free." That felt like a really good question, and when Morgan actually smiled, I knew it was the correct one to ask.

"I will not purchase you, Ava. To bind us makes you a partner. The two of us would be responsible for seeing to the safety and security of this region."

Partner seemed like an awfully big word all of a sudden. There was nothing casual about how she'd said any of that. Yet, her not 'buying' me, as she'd put it, was very interesting. I felt like this was perhaps the way things should be if there was indeed some sort of war coming. And while I was not sure about this whole bit regarding prophecies and me "leading the Supernatural community into the light" as I'd been told was my destiny, I still felt that it was best to have real allies.

"I'll do it." The words that came out of my mouth seemed strange and heavy.

"I am so gonna write about this in the History of Ghouls Tome and Codex," Kayleeni squealed.

"I think this a wise choice, Ava." Race had been silent this entire time. I chose to think it is because he believes I am very capable.

"So what do I do?" I asked in a bit of a rush. "Do I say something, or is there some potion to drink?"

"Nothing like that at all," Morgan said with the slightest hint of a laugh in her voice. "Simply take my hands."

I did as I was told and instantly felt a surge of incredible warmth surge through me and coil in my belly. The warmth began to increase and started to grow towards the point of being uncomfortable.

"Oh," Morgan's voice drifted into my ears from what sounded like a million miles away, "and this might sting just a bit."

That Ghoul Ava Sacks the Quarterback!

11

Hurts So Good

I felt like I was on fire from the inside out. I tried to seek refuge in my special Ava Land, but nothing happened. It seemed like an eternity passed. And then, just as suddenly as it began, it ended.

"What the hell?" I gasped.

I expected Morgan to still be standing right in front of me, but she was all the way across the room and picking herself up off the floor. Kayleeni was looking from me to her; Nose Wart and a bunch of the goblins were actually partway up the stairs and seemed confused. Race was standing beside me; he kept reaching out and then pulling his hands back. It was as if he wanted to touch me but was afraid to do so.

I sent a query inward to check on the denizens of my head. I was relieved to hear everybody respond that nothing at all had changed and that they were fine (except for Boudicca and Butt Pimple who were apparently still locked away securely). I even heard from Mystify and Adrianna which prompted me to hurriedly lock them back away before they could start talking or distract me.

"That was crazy." Kayleeni finally broke the silence as she pulled out what looked like a rolled up magazine. "I don't recall anything like that happening when I bonded. It stung a little, but both of you screamed like you were being gutted and then there was a bright flash followed by this ball of blackness that shrouded you both for like ten seconds before Morgan got blasted across the room. Did the binding fail?"

Morgan slowly got to her feet and brushed herself off. After shaking her head and taking a few unsteady steps, she seemed like nothing had ever happened. Come to think of it...I felt fine. It felt as if the past few moments, or however long, were just a dream. I knew a thing or two about making a quick recovery, but this was really and truly as if nothing had occurred.

"Ava, I need you to do something," Morgan said as she walked to one of my huge couches and sat down. "I need you to focus on B—" She paused suddenly; clipping off whatever she was about to say. After a few seconds, she continued. "I want you to focus on Belinda. Think about her and wonder where she might be."

That seemed kinda strange, but I did as she asked. It wasn't a few heartbeats later that I felt something in my head. Without realizing it, I'd turned to the right.

"Good, now tell her that her presence is required at your home," Morgan said calmly. "Think it, you don't need to say the words. Just think it to that sensation of her being that you feel."

I did. It was strange, but I could feel the confusion coming back to me...and something else.

Fear.

"No, I did not expect her to like that at all," Morgan chuckled.

"So now what?" I asked.

"Belinda will be here shortly. You have summoned her," Morgan said as if that were the entire answer and there was nothing left to be said on the subject.

"Okay, that's all well and good, but we need to do something about Anthony and this Key-oh-hoodly-what's-it." I was proud of myself for not forgetting amidst all this insanity.

"Keyoggia," Race, Morgan, and Kayleeni all said in a chorus of exasperation..

"Sure...whatever." I shrugged, not overly concerned that I

could not remember this ogre magi fella's name.

"All you need to do is concentrate on something that does not belong."

"That doesn't make any sense…" But as the words left my lips, I could feel something that felt plain old wrong. I might compare it to a pebble in your shoe, but it was more than that. "I feel something." I turned slowly until my body was pointed at the source of this odd feeling.

"You can feel him," Morgan said as more of an affirmation. "Which is odd…because up until now, I have not been able to."

"And now?" Race asked.

"He is crystal clear to me. I could probably pinpoint his location to within a few blocks if I looked at a map." She glanced at me. "But with Ava having this connection, there is no need. She could follow her senses to wherever Keyoggia is hiding."

"So I am going after this guy?" I know it seemed like a silly question, but the lack of urgency that everybody was displaying had me wondering.

"Oh yes, you will certainly be dealing with this, but I believe we need to clear the decks between us beforehand."

I was not sure what exactly Morgan was talking about, but the tone in her voice put me on edge right away. She was staring at me and I had a feeling that she could see into my very heart.

"Where is Betty?" Morgan asked simply.

My eyes shot over to Race and then back to Morgan. I was not sure that this was something I felt ready to share with everybody.

"Do we need to do this now?" I asked; my voice a bit of a whine.

"Absolutely," was Morgan's one-word answer.

There is no way around this, Ava, Betty said with a sigh. *You will not be able to hide this from her any longer.*

But what about Race? I struggled not to say that out loud.

There comes a time when you must allow yourself to trust, child, Blodwen spoke up. *I believe the young man has your best interests at heart. He will not betray you.*

I found myself staring at the floor. "She died a couple of

days ago." I let that statement hang in the air. They could imply whatever they wanted from it. Chances are, nobody was gonna be fooled by my not actually saying the words.

"You are wise to keep that information to yourself," Morgan finally said, breaking the silence. "I imagine that she advised you not to tell me when we spoke earlier." It wasn't a question.

"I agree with Morgan," Race added. "You are already considered quite a threat. If they knew that you consumed not only the gwyll, but also one of the most infamous Amazonian shaman priestesses…"

Race was still talking, but I was too stunned to hear anything he said. Instead, my focus was inward.

Really, Betty? Like, Amazonian warrior types? I fired off. *And just how long were you going to keep that little secret?*

When I felt you were ready, I would have told you. There is a lot of power, and you are not prepared for it quite yet. There was no hint of remorse or apology in the woman's tone. *That spell you are struggling with so terribly is one of the first I learned and perhaps one of the most basic. Maybe when you are able to handle that, I will be more willing to teach you more. Power used poorly is almost worse than power used improperly.*

At first I didn't understand what the difference was, then I remembered Adrianna. She was supposedly one of the most gifted necromancers of her time. She had started what history recorded as the Black Plague. There had been a lot of effort to make society forget the true horror of what had happened and see it as some disease spread by rat fleas. I guess I could see her point. After all, it wasn't like she truly knew my mind. All any of the Supernaturals had to go by when it came to female ghouls was the legacy left by Boudicca.

"Ava!" Morgan's voice snapped me back to the moment.

"Huh?"

"That young man is waking." She gave a nod to the entry hall where I'd laid Colt down after we'd come in from battling the trolls.

I walked out to see him sitting up and rubbing his head. He looked up at me and his eyes suddenly went wide with fear. In his efforts to scoot away from me, he ended up falling on the floor. His head bounced off the hardwood with a nasty crack and I actually thought he'd knocked himself back out.

"Y-y-you stay away from me," he stammered.

I didn't get it. He'd seen me in Sharkmouth mode. He'd seen my switch-digits. Why was he suddenly so freaked out?

"Easy, Colt," a sweet voice said from beside me. I glanced down to see that I'd been joined by Kayleeni. "Ava is on your side, remember? Anthony and I hired her to protect you."

"B-b-but she ate that guy!" His eyes were wide and he stared at me in absolute horror. It seemed that he'd at last reached a point where his mind could no longer just dismiss what his eyes were seeing.

"He was dead," I offered. Kayleeni shot me a dirty look that indicated I might not be helping.

"Mr. Faber," Morgan said as she approached. "I regret to inform you that you have been witness to a few things that society is not quite yet ready to digest. Miss Birch is, in fact, a ghoul. That person, or what you believed to be a person, was actually a troll. Much the same as your team mate and friend Mr. Riddle is half-troll. The young lady beside Miss Birch," Morgan gestured to Kayleeni, "is a water elf. As hard as all of this is for you to process, I assure you that it is very true. Unfortunately, you were not supposed to be exposed to any of this. There have been some terrible lapses in judgement by a few individuals, but that can't be helped now. I have two offers for you, and I will give you one minute to choose. Sadly, there will be no other options."

"What sort of options?" Colt asked the question that was on the tip of my tongue.

"The first is that we kill you and then I have Miss Birch here eat the evidence." Colt's face paled and he struggled visibly to swallow the lump in his throat. "The second choice is that you put all of this away and think no more of it for now. There may be a time when it will be okay for you to share what you have witnessed. When that time comes, I do hope that you will remember that Miss Birch has put her life at risk to keep you safe."

As Morgan laid out that second option, Colt began to nod; obviously he had already decided which option was best. His eyes shot past Morgan, and I saw Race stroll in. He watched Colt with curiosity and then smiled.

"I just have to say that I am a huge fan of yours, Colt," my big, strong Templar gushed, sounding a lot like some school girl meeting one of The New Kids on the Block. Sure, I could have come up with something more current, but I am and shall always be an 80's kinda gal.

For some reason, that seemed to shake the young man out of his daze. Colt nodded to Race and stepped around me as if I weren't even there as he reached out and took Race's out-stretched hand. At first I thought that the two were shaking hands, then I saw that the Templar had produced a scrap of paper and a pen.

Men, I sniffed inwardly.

I turned to Kayleeni. "So, we need to come up with a plan to take on this ogre magi thing."

***

"This is sorta nasty," I whispered to Theodore the owlbear.

"I am only surprised that Nose Wart is here for this. It is very uncommon for the male to actually be present for the birth of a litter," Theodore replied.

I heard another yelp from the large nest of torn up rags that was apparently the birthing bed for Teat Mucous. Nose Wart popped up on his tiptoes and looked over the edge. A smile crossed his face.

"Another boy, Just Ava!" he chirped. "That makes seven males and only one female. I will certainly find one strong enough to step into my shoes when my time has come to an end."

That seemed like an odd thing to say. I had never given any thought to Nose Wart being gone, much less dying.

A goblin has a life span of about nine years, Betty said.

"How old are you, Nose Wart?" I asked as casually as I

could after stepping up beside him.

"I have no idea," the little goblin shrugged.

Well that didn't help. I stepped back as the birthing process continued. When it was all said and done, Teat Mucous brought thirteen mewling, fussy little goblins into the world. Also, and this was when I had to excuse myself, three stillborns arrived. These were to be shared by the parents. And when I say shared…I mean…well, you know.

"Do you still have a location for Keyoggia?" Kayleeni asked as I shut the door to the lower level and made my way to the living room.

The water elf was sitting in the living room with two bugbears. From the looks of it, they were playing some sort of game that involved dice and a dagger. One of the bugbears was bleeding from a puncture on his left foot and I scowled at the blood that had pooled on my floor.

"Yep." I was still curious as to why nobody seemed to be in a big hurry to rescue Anthony.

"Okay, and I take it he hasn't gone anywhere?" Kayleeni rolled the dice and then snatched up the dagger. She spun around in circles twice and, with her eyes closed, threw that wicked blade at one of the bugbears. The big creature was seated on the floor with his legs apart and the dagger plunged into the floor right between those legs. Another inch and there would likely be no little bugbears produced by the giant, furry beast.

I was only in shock for a second, but then I snapped out of it. "What the hell are you doing to my floor?" I yelled.

Kayleeni looked up at me with an expression of confusion. The bugbears were a different story. They cringed and both started to their feet, looks of worry showing as their massive eyebrows drooped and their whiskers began to quiver.

"Your floor?" the water elf sounded confused.

Okay, maybe I should be more concerned that she'd just barely missed turning one of my bugbears into a eunuch, but these hardwood floors are gorgeous and damned if I was going to have them all gouged up with daggers.

"Oh…I get it." Kayleeni held up a hand to forestall my next

outburst.

She hurried over to the gouge and knelt beside it. A sweet song escaped her lips and she passed her hands over the gash where the dagger had driven into the wood. When her hand came away, the floor was as good as new.

"Neat trick," I grumbled. "But that still doesn't take care of the blood all over my floor."

Okay, I probably should have been more concerned with the bugbear's leg. I only briefly wondered if I was acting more like a human or a Supernatural. Then, one of the bugbears growled something and pointed to the main part of the mess. His bushy eyebrows raised and the tufted ears sort of twitched a bit. I had no idea what he was trying to convey so I just shrugged and nodded.

I guess I should not have been surprised when the seven-plus foot tall thing dropped to all fours and lapped up every single drop of blood. When it finished, it stood and ducked its head a bit as if to ask if it was good enough.

"Yeah...that'll do," I said, my lips pursed and then turned my attention back to Kayleeni. "You are awfully relaxed for somebody whose friend has been abducted and is being held prisoner by an ogre magi thingy."

"They don't want Anthony, they want you. He is bait...but you are an actual ghoul...a *female*." The way that Kayleeni said female was sort of strange. There was a lot of what sounded like awe and even reverence. People were really expecting a great deal of results from me. As always, I wish that I shared their confidence.

"And I am going to do everything that I can to get him back. So why are we waiting? Why don't we simply go and get him back?" I asked what I considered a pretty obvious question.

"We have not heard from Keyoggia. We have no idea what his conditions are going to be."

"Well, the team has a game tomorrow and they need Anthony. I am not just going to sit around and wait for them to make the first move. I think I heard it somewhere that it is better to act than to react."

112

I turned and headed to my chiller. If I was going to go to battle, I needed to eat first and then bring along a few spares just in case.

"Nose Wart?" I called.

In an instant, the goblin was beside me. "Yes, Just Ava?"

I could see that he was anxious and distracted. It dawned on me that I'd just pulled him to me and away from the brand new baby goblins. I have no idea what sorts of things goblins do with their newborns...probably teach them to spit so they can curse properly or some such non-human thing.

"Can you accompany me? I am going after Anthony and that means a probable fight with the ogre magus." As soon as I asked, I felt like a total jerk, but on the positive side, I knew the singular form of ogre magi...so, yay me!

"I am always at your service, Just Ava." Nose Wart bowed at the waist, but I saw something in his expression.

Odd, I have never known goblins to be the doting parental sort, Blodwen whispered.

Yes, a very human...un-goblin sort of reaction, Betty added.

"I need you to assemble me a team of ten of your most fierce and trusted goblins," I commanded.

"Right away, Just Ava." The little goblin scampered through the door leading to the lower levels and vanished.

Less than five minutes later, a band of armed goblins were lining up before me. Standing at the ready, Nose Wart presented me with his choices.

"If you were not here, which of these goblins would you say is the best to step into your place?" I asked, walking up and down the line and trying to figure out where in the hell they came up with their odd variety of weapons. One of them was holding what looked like a giant version of an egg beater, but it was sporting nasty coils of what resembled barbed wire on steroids.

"I would think that Knee Ooze would be the best fighter besides myself." Nose Wart gestured and a goblin stepped forward. In his hands he held a barbed dagger in one and what looked like a Frisbee ringed with rusty razor blades in the other.

"Then he shall accompany me and you shall stay here," I announced.

With a moan that sounded as if he was about to hurl, Nose Wart threw himself at my feet. "How have I failed in my service to you, Mistress?"

Tread careful here, Ava. If the other goblins sense there is an opportunity, Nose Wart might find himself facing challenges from those who aspire to lead the clan, Blodwen warned.

"You have done nothing. You still lead the clan of Just Goblins." I had to stifle a chuckle as I said the new tribe name. "My home may very well come under attack, and I need the best of you to have all the forces assembled and ready to fight."

Nose Wart gave me a curious glance and I shot him a wink. I wasn't sure if he would understand, but there was that human side of me again.

Five minutes later, I was pulling out of my garage. It had been awhile since I'd been able to take my precious Corvette out for a spin.

Kayleeni was in the passenger seat, her smile wide as her eyes scanned the dashboard. "Thanks for letting me ride with you instead of the Templar," the water elf gushed.

"It was either you, or I had to stuff a bunch of goblins in my car. I've traveled in confined spaces with the little gas bags before…no thanks. Let Race deal with that."

I turned on my car's stereo system and dialed in my favorite Sirius channel: Hair Nation. The timing could not have been better…Brett was teasing me with a little *Unskinny Bop.*

I focused on that feeling in my gut as I hit the interstate. We were heading towards the industrial district down by the river. As I sang at the top of my lungs, I prepared myself for a fight. If these people wanted a war…I could sure as hell give them one.

12

Hit Me with Your Best Shot

I drove up to what looked to be some sort of shipping yard with the giant cranes that have the massive spotlights on them. I could see workers driving around forklifts and all sorts of regular dockworker sorts of things going on. I saw a strip of parking spots and pulled into the one farthest from all the other cars. I could absolutely walk a few extra steps if it meant keeping the paint job on my beautiful car from getting a bunch of dings.

I motioned for Race to go to the far end of the parking lot. He pulled up in his van behind where I'd parked; I could see he had the window rolled down.

"You did that on purpose." He shot a nasty look over his shoulder at what I was sure had to be the little band of goblins. "And you are sure this is the place?"

"My gut says so." I smiled as Knee Ooze jumped up onto the passenger seat of the van and gave me a salute with his odd little weapon.

"Okay, you go in from up here and I will make my way in at the other end. I should be able to find you quick enough."

"Security activated," a voice said from my car as I pushed the button on the fob to lock it up.

"You sure?" I asked dubiously.

"Sure…I'll just follow the screaming." He flashed me a

115

crooked smile that would've made Han Solo jealous and then drove away.

"This seems like a strange place for Keyoggia to bring Anthony," Kayleeni said as we crossed the road and approached the tall security fence that ran the length of this facility.

"This seems like the perfect place." I paused and let my gut do its thing. I could feel the presence of the ogre magus creature beyond the big fenced off area that marked the loading docks.

"How so?" The water elf sniffed and made a face. "And what have they done to that poor river?"

"Haven't you ever been to the Willamette?" I asked. "How can you have lived in Portland and not been to this river?"

"You didn't pay attention to your program," Kayleeni replied with a laugh. "Anthony is from Texas. We both lived near San Antonio."

I guess I had never thought about it. "So where do you guys live?"

"The team put us all up in a big apartment complex that the general manager actually owns. Of course the only water there was the pool." She screwed up her face and gave an over-exaggerated shudder. "Chlorine...nasty stuff. I don't understand humans at all. They say they are keeping water clean by adding poison to it."

"Yeah, well the Willamette could use a few thousand gallons of the stuff," I mumbled.

"That's another thing...why do all of the places around here have to be so complicated to say? I was in the airport when we arrived...I just mentioned that I was excited to visit this state called Ory-gone. Some kid working in the coffee cart said that it is pronounced Ory-*gun*. Then he gave us a short version of proper pronunciations for places tourists like to visit. One of them was the Willamette. He said that if we got in a taxi and asked to go to the Wil-a-met river...the cabbie would laugh at us. Willam-*ut*...he even made us practice saying it as he made our coffees."

"Yeah, this state has a bit of a complex when it comes to our names and how we pronounce them." I stopped at the fence and looked around; my main search was for security types. "Can you jump?" I asked when I saw that we were in an area that was pretty clear of any sort of traffic.

"Like this?" Kayleeni hopped a few inches off the ground.

"No…this." And then I bounded over the twelve-foot high fence topped with three strands of razor wire, landing softly on the balls of my feet on the other side.

"Umm…nope." The water elf shook her head vigorously. "We can swim like fish, but water elves aren't much for jumping."

I jumped back to her side and turned to offer her my back. "Hold on tight, it will only take a second."

"Maybe I could find another way around?" Kayleeni's voice had become suddenly timid to the point where the tremor crept in at the end making what had started off as a statement into a question.

"Is there a problem?"

"No…w-w-why would you say that?" The water elf actually took a few steps away from me.

"An old Jedi mind trick," I snickered. "That, or the fact that you are sweating like you just ran a marathon."

"It's just that…well…water elves are not big on flying."

"You won't be flying. I will be jumping and you will be holding on to me for just a couple of seconds while we move from here," I pointed at the ground where we stood, "to there." I pointed at the shadowy area on the other side of the fence.

"You make it sound so easy." Kayleeni did not sound very convinced.

"Okay, then you stay here and I will be back as soon as I am done dealing with this Keyoggia." I turned to jump over and head towards where the warm tingle in my belly indicated.

"Wait," came the strangled cry. "Maybe if I just shut my eyes."

"Whatever works for you."

Alright, while I didn't exactly see what her big hang-up was over the whole jumping the fence thing, one thing I would not do is dismiss somebody's fear or phobia or whatever it is. I had friends who were afraid of clowns, cramped spaces, open spaces…and spiders. We all have something that sets us on edge. Who was I to give the little water elf grief over her fear of leaving the ground?

I knelt so that she could get a grip around my neck. Instantly, I was very glad that I did not need to breathe. If I did, she would have choked me out before I could get back to my feet.

"We are gonna go on the count of three," I said calmly. "One…two…" And then I jumped.

I landed and heard a strange sound behind me. I was afraid that I might've given Kayleeni a heart attack or something.

"Oh…do that again!" she breathed. "That was amazing."

We hadn't really gone that far or that high. I knew from experience that I could really cover some distance when I jumped. The thing is, we simply did not have the time at the moment.

"How about later?" I knelt so she could slip off my back. I felt her reluctance, but she did as I'd asked.

I gathered my bearings and then turned in the direction that I felt the pull coming from. We stuck to the shadows as we moved, not wanting to draw any attention to ourselves.

At last, we reached a long building that was about the length of a football field and thirty or so feet high. A new smell drifted into my nostrils. It was joined by another that was familiar, and I paused at the single metal door that I knew to be the way to go if I was going to deal with this ogre magus. A third new smell came on the heels of the first two and I was actually becoming confused.

It isn't that I am not used to various smells. But, for instance, all humans have a very basic smell that is enhanced by your closeness to death (real, not perceived, so it isn't like I would know if you were about to walk out in front of a car or something). These were absolutely Supernaturals. Three very different ones in close proximity.

One of them reminded me of smoke and some sort of exotic spice. There was a bitter tanginess to it that almost tickled my nose. The familiar one was Anthony. The third was the one that really had me confused. It smelled…dirty. Foul. There was a serious wrongness to it that made me almost hurt. I can't explain it any better than that.

"What's wrong?" Kayleeni whispered.

Almost on cue, and like something from a really bad horror flick, the side door to the warehouse opened of its own accord. The hinges even made a tiny squeak in protest. I was strangely less confident all of a sudden.

"Well, so much for the element of surprise," I grumbled.

I stepped through the door. As I started up the long hall that terminated in another metal door, I willed my switch-digits and Sharkmouth into being.

"I love it when you do that," Kayleeni whispered.

We reached the door and stopped. I waited for a moment to see if it would open like the previous one, but nothing happened. Whatever I was smelling was right on the other side of this door.

"Maybe we should go get Race." Kayleeni took a step back. She had just voiced my exact thoughts.

Wait, I thought. *I am more than capable. I have faced off with some pretty nasty beasties and I'm still standing. I'm a ghoul, dammit. Every member of the Supernatural community fears me to some extent. I would be willing to bet that even Morgan has a little bit of concern hidden under that calm façade.*

"I'm going in." And with those three simple words, I opened the door and stepped into what looked like a massive shipment storage area.

"Ava Birch." Standing in the middle of the enormous open floor area of the warehouse was a creature that stood easily ten feet tall. He had greenish-gray skin with swatches of blue. His hair was jet black and pulled up on top of his head in a topknot that was very Gene Simmons-esque. He had a smallish head for his huge body and there was sort of a reverse sabre-tooth tiger thing going on with a pair of massive tusk/teeth jutting from his lower jaw. Personally, I didn't see how he could have survived and not punctured his own cheeks with those things.

"You must be Keyoggia," I said, trying to sound unimpressed.

He made a bow, throwing the purple and gold kimono thing

he was wearing out in a flourish. I noticed that he was sporting a blue sumo-wrestler style thong or diaper whats-a-ma-bob underneath. I'm sure somebody knows what those things are called, but they always reminded me of a diaper.

Okay, so there was the source of the odd spice sort of smell I was picking up on. I did not see Anthony anywhere. Also, I did not see the source of that dark scent that had me knotting up a bit in my belly. And not in the good way that I do whenever I see Race.

"I expected you to be...taller." Keyoggia made a derisive snort and scratched his braided jet black beard. The boys of ZZ Top would have been a little impressed. It was easily a foot long and had all sorts of beads and stuff braided into it. I was hit by an image of Bo Derek running in slow motion across a beach towards the adorable Dudley Moore. And if you don't have any idea what I'm referring to in that image...you have my pity.

"That line is getting old," I scoffed. "And leave it to a male to think that size matters."

Okay...it does matter some. But an enthusiastic lover can often make up for it as long as we aren't talking Inch-High Private Eye. Oh, and fellas, yes...there is also such a thing as too much. Just because we can pass a baby does not mean we enjoy the feeling of something the size of...well...we can discuss this later. Right now, I have a butt kicking to attend.

"So, where's Anthony?" I asked. It wasn't that I actually expected an answer, but you never know unless you ask.

"He is close, but that is not really why you are here, is it?" Keyoggia asked. His big, leathery lips curled up into a smile that made him even less attractive if that were possible.

"Actually, it is exactly why I am here. I just figure killing you and ridding Morgan's territory of an unwelcome invader will be a bonus." I took another step closer, but my eyes were scanning the area. There was still that unknown being hiding someplace.

"Do you have any idea what you are messing with?" the ogre made a sound in his chest that was presumably a laugh.

"I seldom do, I think that is why I do so well. Maybe if I

knew more, then I would overthink the situation." Okay, so overthinking was never something that I would probably be accused of any time soon (if ever), but he didn't have to know that.

"I hear you usually stumble into things and luck hands you most of your victories." Again the huge creature made that sound that I was now certain had to be a laugh. It actually sounded like a muted earthquake; and yes, earthquakes make a sound. I've been in a couple...so there. Oh, and maybe he knew more about me than I initially supposed.

"And are you gonna introduce me to whoever this friend is that is hiding someplace nearby?" I called that out to be sure that whoever this was that remained hidden would be aware that I knew it (can't really say 'he' or 'she' yet) was present.

"No need to yell, Miss Avangelina Katherine Birch," a voice whispered. Only, that wasn't really correct. It was not so much a whisper as it was a projection. It almost felt like the voice was inside my head, but I was too stunned to pay that much attention.

I have not been called by my full name for over twenty years. (And don't start trying to do the math to figure out my age...that's just rude.) As for my middle name, I didn't think anybody knew it. In fact, it was not even on my driver's license. I'd had my birth certificate changed when I was eighteen. Katherine was my mother's name, and I'd made a point to erase as much of her footprint from my life as possible as soon as I was legally able to do so. Not even my ex-husband knew my middle name.

Both Betty and Blodwen were starting to kick up a bit of a fuss. The problem was that they were basically talking over each other and it was not a distraction that I needed at the moment. I slammed them away to help clear my head. Perhaps that wasn't the best choice, but I really did not have the time or the patience to deal with their distractions at the moment.

"You must be the mystery guest," I managed as my mouth went dry.

Whoa! My mouth never did that, I thought.

"At last we meet," the voice cooed.

At the far end of the warehouse, the thing that stepped out was...magnificent. If Keyoggia was ten feet tall, then this thing was at least twelve. The thing was, he looked human...at first glance.

Okay, take away the twelve feet tall aspect and he looked human. Mostly. Sort of. Then my eyes began to take in the details. For one, his long hair that was a good several inches past his shoulders was silver. And when I say silver, I mean that, if somebody spun actual silver into fine strands and created a wig, then this is what it would look like. The thing is, I knew this was not just a wig. His skin was a solid ebony color but the veins that ran underneath were the color of molten lava. It was really striking actually. The toga he wore was a shade of emerald green that shone and sparkled like it might really be made from thousands of the precious stones.

His face was beautiful. This is that beauty that James Belushi warned Rob Lowe of in *About Last Night*. And if you have not had the pleasure of sitting through that opening scene where the catch lines are:

Rob's character: "Was she a pro?"

Jim's character: "At this point, we don't know."

Well then...you have my pity.

The only thing that was off kilter rested in the wraparound dark shades that this whatever-it-was currently wore. Something told me that those eyes would be a sight to behold.

"At last we meet?" I scoffed. "That is sorta cheesy, isn't it? I mean, if you are the big, bad beastie that I am meeting for the first time, shouldn't you have a better opening line?"

"So much of the modern mind is wasted on senseless drivel that passes for entertainment. Avangelina Katherine Birch, perhaps your mind is one of the most underused and banal that I have had the misfortune of encountering." The giant creature laughed, but unlike Keyoggia's, this one was melodic and sweet. It did not fit the nastiness in its tone just a second earlier as it rattled off that last insult.

"So, this is going to seem like a silly question." I glanced over at Keyoggia and then returned my attention to the creature that I now assumed to be in charge. "Who, and perhaps more importantly, *what* are you?" I was still puzzling over the name he kept spewing from his perfect lips. I wasn't about to let him know that it bothered me, though. That would be perhaps tipping my hand a bit. There was something about this thing's knowledge that reminded me of something...maybe a book or a movie?

"I will credit you with deciding that what I am is more important than who...to a point. So let's start with the 'what' portion of your question." He smiled big, showing off perfect and dazzling teeth. I noted that there weren't any fangs. That had to be good, right?

"Before you start, can I ask if all of your answers are going to be as drawn out? Seriously, get over the sound of your voice. Am I right, Kayleeni?" I glanced down to the water elf.

Okay, to be more specific, I glanced down to where I thought the water elf would be standing. She'd been right by my side as far as I knew. Imagine my surprise when I looked down to see that I was entirely alone.

"Your little friend exercised her common sense," Keyoggia guffawed. It was an ugly sound coming from the creature that, especially since he stood in contrast to this gorgeous thing at the end of the warehouse with the musical voice, made me want to end him all that much sooner.

"It must suck for you," I said coolly, turning my gaze to the ogre magus. It cocked its tiny head to the side in obvious confusion. "To be the ugly one of the team. Seriously, if the two of you hang out on the side, I bet you just hate how the female...whatevers that come around all flock to him and leave you standing outside the room staring at the tie dangling from the doorknob."

"I am going to enjoy ripping you limb-from-limb, bitch," Keyoggia spat.

Good, I thought. I'd struck a nerve. That meant he would be perhaps a bit over-eager if/when he and I fought.

"Keyoggia, do not be so easily manipulated. You are supposed to the smarter breed of the ogre species. Stop acting like your idiot brethren."

There was nothing gentle in the scolding that was dished out to the ogre, and I saw it cast me an even angrier glare just before bowing its head.

"As you say, my master," Keyoggia muttered grudgingly.

"Master?" I burst out, not trying to stifle my laugh even a little bit. "Your role in this situation just keeps getting funnier."

"I think it is best that you keep your conversation between you and I for now," the bigger creature warned.

"Fine, then tell me your name so I know what to call you other than the tall dude." I planted my hands on my hips and leveled my gaze on the creature after making it a point to give what I hoped was a very dismissive look of disgust tinged with just a bit of amusement in Keyoggia's direction.

"Very well, but I will give you what you ask after I offer up this warning. Once I've answered, you and I will start down a road that cannot be circumvented. It will end in death...yours being the most likely," the glorious creature spoke. I heard something in his voice that made me pause. It wasn't malice or anything wicked, it was almost sad.

I've gotten by on just doing things by the seat of my pants for a while. I was not so foolish as to believe that that wouldn't bite me on that very same seat one of these days.

"I think it is only fair that I know who my enemy is," I responded with as much confidence as I could muster—which was not nearly as much as I'd felt when this encounter first began.

"Vinwoanoch," it said, dropping into a low bow. That is when I saw the massive wings unfurl.

"Okay...so say that again a bit slower, it was kinda jumbled." I had walked close enough that I was now just a few strides from Keyoggia.

"It is actually a newer translation from Akkadian, a language that has been dead for over fifteen hundred years. And my original name pre-dates even that."

"You haven't answered my question. If you don't care how bad I mangle it, then fine..." I let that statement hang, counting on this creature's vanity to give me what I needed.

"Vine-who-ah-nock," he said as he rose once more to his full height. "And, for now, this is where we must part ways."

"Oh no you don't," I snapped. "You still haven't told me what the blazes you are."

"You haven't figured it out, Avangelina Katherine Birch?"

I winced. There it was, slapping me in the face. A piece of my life that I'd buried long ago. I'd been confident that it was gone for good.

"I am one of the Fallen." Vinwoanoch held his head just a little higher. His hair fluttered like somebody had directed a fan on him and his wings went wide, spanning at least thirty feet.

There was a loud pop like a pistol being fired, and then a nasty smell that was like electricity and sulfur...heavy on the sulfur. And with just a slight puff of smoke remaining to ever give evidence that there had even been anything there, he...it was gone.

You foolish girl! Blodwen stormed. *You have exchanged names with one of the Fallen.*

I guess I'd let my mind slip a bit because suddenly I felt Betty, Blodwen, and even Cody out of their containment in my head. Cody was confused, but Betty and Blodwen were furious.

The Fallen...like in angels? I asked skeptically.

Also known as demons, Betty stated clinically.

I was about to ponder what all of that meant when I felt something slam into me like a dump truck hitting a Yugo...with me being the Yugo. I had forgotten all about Keyoggia. That was a mistake that could be fatal.

That Ghoul Ava Sacks the Quarterback!

13

Here I Go Again

"My rise to power begins here, ghoul," the ogre spat. "Vin-woanoch will seat me in a position of great power after I dispose of you."

I stood up and had to shove the chunks of splintered pallets that I'd been thrown into off my body. The good news was that I was now a good fifty feet away from Keyoggia.

The ogre magus made a gesture and a ball of flames appeared to dance between his hands. He raised them above his head and then flung both arms out towards me sending the fireball my way. As it flew in a bee-line for me, the sphere grew until it was the size of a large beach ball. I just barely managed to dive to the side as it hit the splintered pile of pallets. There was a wave of heat and suddenly there was a bonfire roaring where I had been standing only a few heartbeats ago.

"You are nothing but a bootlicking lackey," I retorted as I scanned the room and planned my attack. "And if you think that just beating me is going to get you anywhere, then you might be just as stupid as a regular ogre."

Apparently that was a nasty insult to the ogre magi sort. He let out a roar and drew a triple extra-large version of a samurai sword. I did not need to be close to know that blade was very sharp. In just four strides, Keyoggia was on me and bringing his sword around in a swipe that I had to Matrix dodge to avoid.

Before he could come around with the return swing, I brought my left leg out in a wheel kick that forced him to leap back and recover, completely ruining his second attempt to cleave me in half. I leapt straight up and landed on a crossbeam that ran across the width of this warehouse.

As Keyoggia spun towards me, I saw another ball of nastiness roiling from the fingertips of his left hand. Streams of absolute blackness shot in my general direction but went well wide. When those strands hit the roof, there was a sizzling noise. That area of the roof was simply gone.

Negative energy, Betty hissed. *It will simply eradicate anything it comes into contact with.*

Good to know, I managed as I bounded down four more of the crossbeams in an attempt to get behind the spell casting ogre.

I reached the fourth beam and then stepped off, basically jumping to the ground. I landed behind a pair of really large forklifts and took a deep breath to try and gather my wits.

"Yes, fight...struggle...make this a delicious kill," Keyoggia crooned.

"And you really think that demon is going to reward you?" I tried to sound mocking. "I think he is just letting you take all the risk. He bailed instead of trying to face off with me. I think he knows that I am gonna kick your butt, and he just wants to try and get a better idea of my capabilities." I was rattling off the reply, basically paraphrasing what Blodwen was saying in my head.

Seriously, you didn't think that I would jump to a conclusion like that on my own do you? If so, then you really haven't been paying attention.

I threw myself flat as I heard something hurl my direction. A blast of cold swished by overhead. When it stopped, I looked up to see that the forklifts were basically frozen. With a tentative swipe of my right hand, the upper cabs shattered into tiny crystals.

"Neat trick," I said with genuine appreciation. Seriously, to freeze metal to the point where it shatters? That is damn cold.

I could see one tree trunk-sized leg as I threw myself flat just as another cone of cold slammed into the body of the fork-lift. Some of that energy flowed under and I barely turned away in time to avoid catching it in the face.

Knowing that he'd dialed in this latest location, I popped up and jumped again. It wasn't until I landed that I realized a good portion of the hair on the back of my head was still on the floor where it'd frozen solid.

It was time to turn the tables and attack. He was almost directly below me as I pounced. Both feet found his back and cut nasty grooves into his flesh on the way down. I was standing right behind Keyoggia and swiped out with both hands in a move I modeled after the Predator monster from the movies. Only my left hand made contact, but it was enough to basically sever the left triceps of the ogre in half. Blood sprayed in a pretty purple jet.

Keyoggia howled and staggered away, spinning my direction and shouting something in a language that sounded sort Latin-y. Darkness shrouded me, and I froze in place momentarily. Normally, darkness means nothing to me. I see as well in the dead of night as you do in the middle of the day. The problem was that, for the first time since I'd become a ghoul, I was actually blind. I was in pitch black and could not see my hand in front of my face.

Magical darkness negates any ability to see, Betty coached. *It is usually a sphere in a set place. The size of the sphere is predicated on the degree of magic the caster is capable of wielding.*

That was easy enough to circumvent. Once more I jumped; this time straight up. Sure enough, I emerged from the dark. but Keyoggia had used the moment to move as well. I'd thought to land on him again and give him a nasty set of switch-toe grooves down his body; instead, I simply landed on the concrete floor.

Keyoggia held his sword one-handed and was in a pose that reminded me of Olympic fencers. I waited for the next spell to be hurled, but nothing came.

He may have exhausted what his essence is capable of ex-

pending until he can recover. He will be reduced to magic that is little more than parlor tricks until that time, Betty told me.

I started to move to my left and he matched me. As we circled, we began the slow process of inching closer to each other. We were within a few more slow steps of this dance when a loud boom came from my right. The sound of a door being thrown open and slamming into the wall caused both me and the ogre to pause.

"Ava!" Race cried.

The goblins poured in from behind him, two pairs carrying a corpse between them. The last to file in was Kayleeni.

"Stay back!" I snapped. "I got this."

"So, "Keyoggia said in his rumbling voice, "you display honor. Then it will be a pleasure to battle you, Ava Birch."

Huh, I thought, *if I didn't know better, I would say that this ogre fella just gave me a compliment.*

Something slid across the floor and I glanced down to see one of the corpses sprawled on the concrete. Up until that moment, I hadn't realized that the back of my head stung terribly. Somehow, I'd blocked out the pain without songs or anything.

I will not allow you to die by any hand other than my own, Boudicca's voice called from somewhere down a dark corridor in a corner of my mind.

I did not have time to ponder how she'd done anything, but I could feel something else when my senses briefly locked onto her. She was weakened. That would be worth remembering. Sadly, I did not have the luxury of time at the moment. Keyoggia took a huge step to cut me off from my potential sustenance.

He had not thought his move through and that step put him with his entire right side to me. I lunged and drove my fingers into his side. As I jumped back to avoid his counterstrike, I heard the pitter patter of several sets of little feet. I'd told Race to stay out of my fight, but apparently the goblins felt that they were exempt.

"Wha—" was all the giant creature had a chance to exclaim before he was laid into by my horde of savage minions.

There was absolutely no way that I would let them get in the kill shot. I charged, expecting the ogre to be so occupied that my strike would be unblocked. I did not account for his ability to basically shake like a dog and send the goblins flying in every direction like massive, meaty water drops. One of those drops caught me square in the stomach and folded me like a lawn chair.

I ended up on my back with a goblin looking down at me. It blinked once and then scrambled off and threw itself on the ground. A pair of legs appeared on either side of my head and I looked up to see Race smiling down at me.

"Need a hand up?" He reached down.

I scowled up at him and slapped his offered hand aside. "I said I got this," I growled between clenched teeth.

He stepped back, throwing his hands up. "It absolutely looks like it. You have him right where you want him. And for the record, I was only offering you a hand to your feet."

I popped up and felt something wrong. Glancing down, it seemed that I had a rib poking through the skin on the right. I guess that little goblin-shaped cannonball had inflicted a tad more damage than I'd realized.

"Mistress!" a goblin called. I turned to see a pair stumping towards me as fast as their tiny legs could manage. They had one of the corpses.

It was like a person who has been stranded in the desert stumbling across a watering hole. I fell to my knees and had lopped off an arm before they even managed to drop the body and move away. I shot a look over at the ogre who was currently swatting away a trio of goblins that had recovered quicker than the others and charged back in.

As I ate, I took in the fight between the ogre and my goblins. This was the sort of behavior that I expected from the little guys and gals. Sadly, there was simply no way they could stand up to ogre magi. The goblins were like gnats to such creatures. The thing is, you could not tell that their charges were in absolute futility by the way they barked and growled and rushed in. Each time, their attacks were rebuffed. Also, I noticed that fewer goblins were getting back to their feet each time. By the time I'd consumed the corpse, even the pair that had served it to me had rushed into the fray. Now...none of them remained. I did not know if they were all dead, or if some might be unconscious. I definitely smelled death in the air and a strand of saliva dripped from the corner of my mouth before I could wipe it away with my sleeve.

"Shall we resume our dance?" Keyoggia turned to face me. I saw his eyes flick to Race for just an instant. Apparently he was satisfied with what he saw, because his gaze quickly returned to me and locked on my eyes.

"Are you sure you are ready to die for some demon?" I asked as we closed and began to circle each other once more.

"You really do not understand, do you?" Keyoggia feinted with his sword. I noticed him wince when he did, a fresh trickle of his purplish blood oozing from the numerous cuts and gouges that marked his body.

"I guess I am gonna go with no," I answered with a shake of my head.

"You represent the potential for the demise of the existence of every Supernatural. If you also possess the powers that are rumored and spoken of in the legends, then you would become the greatest threat in existence if we managed to beat down the humans."

"And why would you have to beat down the humans? Why not try to live with them in peace?"

This caused Keyoggia to throw his tiny head back and emit an ugly laugh. "Do you not pay attention to these creatures? They are distilled hatred. As a species, they are filled with an over-abundance of prejudice and evil for such short lives. You would think they might see their own frailties. Instead, they seem to revel in war and violence. They are constantly looking to dominate and control. What do you think they would do if they realized that the world they have convinced themselves to be fiction is far more real?"

Having not been that far removed from my days as a human, I tried to imagine. That is when it hit me. Suddenly, I understood why I was constantly being accused of thinking like a human.

I think I actually staggered.

Could the human version of me stand face-to-face with ogre magi, vampires, lamias, Valkyries…and demons? My house was a fortress constructed by elves and laden with magical security that vaporized any who sought to do me harm.

I had a horde of goblins (that were growing exponentially as the females popped out litters almost weekly it seemed) that were prepared to die for me. A trio of giants, a few dozen bug-bears (that seemed to add to their numbers monthly in some mysterious way), an owlbear, and a siren all call my residence their home.

"Interesting," Keyoggia said as he paused in our circle of death that was simply delaying the inevitable demise of one of us. "You truly do not understand. You are not yet free of your humanity and refuse to see the bigger picture. You call me a lackey and a pawn of a demon…but what does that make you? How much of what you have done is of your own free will?"

"I would love to keep talking, but I am afraid I have some answers that I need to obtain." I lunged, my hands feinting high and then dropping under his long slender blade at the last second.

I had made it inside his guard and my hands plunged into his belly. With a fierce slice, both hands exited the body in a shower of gore. Something plunged into my left shoulder and I felt a brief sensation of pain.

It was very brief because I drove my face into the open gash across the belly of Keyoggia and bit into the strong, throbbing muscle that was the creature's heart. I felt a rush of life pour into me as it left the ogre magus. A swirl of energy danced before my eyes as I let Sharkmouth devour impossibly large chunks.

I have no idea how long it took, and my next moment of lucidity found me sitting in the middle of the floor of the massive warehouse. There was little sign that Keyoggia had ever existed except for a dark smear on the concrete.

Race was standing several feet away with Kayleeni. Two goblins were just behind him. Both looked horrible, one of them holding an arm with at least two extra elbow joints and the other bleeding from the mouth, ears, and nose.

"We need to get you home," the Templar said emotionlessly. "The sun will be coming up in a little over an hour."

Wow, how long had it taken to eat Keyoggia? I wondered. *And will he—*

The rumors are true, a new voice said from inside my head.

14

Emotional Rescue

A loud clatter made me jump. We'd barely arrived home as the first washes of color were pushing back the darkness of night. The house had been totally quiet, which was more than a little peculiar considering the variety of Supernatural residents that also called it home.

"Sorry, Just Ava," a tiny voice squawked.

I turned to see Nose Wart standing on the counter in my kitchen. He was pulling out a large pan about the size that you would roast a turkey in.

"What are you doing?" I asked, perhaps sounding a bit harsher than I should.

"Thumb Sliver's mate was one of the bodies you returned home with and I am simply gathering up all the bits to take down to his surviving beloved. She was most grateful when she heard that he was one of those who were given the honor of your transporting them to their mates." The goblin paused and then a sparkle appeared in his eyes. "You thought this might have something to do with the wee goblins, didn't you?"

I couldn't deny that it did so I just kept staring at him with as little emotion on my face as possible. He and his mate had already explained that the stillborn babes were to be devoured and that it would impart strength to the next litter so that perhaps

135

fewer would be born dead. Whether that had even the slightest hint of truth to it, I had no idea.

"She is the last, as was her station in the tribe, so this will be the final time I have to come up to retrieve a body. All the rest have been removed from the garage," Nose Wart reported.

I watched him waddle past me and through the living room and into the garage. I heard the door open and a moment later shut. When he stumped back into the kitchen and opened the door leading down to the lower levels carrying an obviously heavy roasting pan, he didn't say a word.

He has grown comfortable around you in a way I did not believe possible, Blodwen said.

Yeah, well, we need to get back to discussing this demon, I snapped.

Had you not exchanged names with one of the Fallen, we would have no need to discuss any of this, Betty harrumphed.

I didn't believe that for a moment, and if they were as smart as they claimed—and I believed—then they didn't either. All this talk about the start of a war should be proof enough. And if not, then all they needed to do was cobble together the bits and pieces we were absolutely sure about and the rest filled in nicely.

Vinwoanoch was in Morgan's territory without permission. He made it very clear that the ball is rolling, and I believe that the first shots were fired tonight, I said to the pair.

But that does not answer anything about why a human was brought in to this nonsense, Betty pressed. *I simply refuse to believe that human sports are important to anybody in the Supernatural community.*

"Nothing back yet on Vinwoanoch," Race announced as he entered the room. "And Anthony seems fine. He and Kayleeni are heading back to his place."

"So, maybe you can offer up a theory," I said as I turned my attention to the Templar that was currently standing shirtless in the doorway to the lower levels of my home, a single goblin peering from behind one leg for some odd reason.

"On?" He glanced down at the goblin and made a shooing gesture. The tiny creature scurried away, but as soon as his attention was focused on me, it moved right back up beside his leg.

"I still can't figure out what Colt has to do with any of this. He is a human. If I was the target, there are a million better ways to lure me out than this."

"Have you thought to ask Keyoggia?" he replied.

"What makes you so sure that he is residing in my head?"

"It was just a guess until this second," Race said with a laugh. "If he wasn't, you would have just come out and said so. The fact that you instantly got defensive tells me that it's pretty likely considering how you were about Betty. Oh…and you have that same look on your face like you are trying to look more innocent than you really ever could hope to be."

"You think you're so smart." I turned my back on him and headed down one of my sunless hallways to an upstairs room that possessed no windows.

"I am *so* smart," Race said as he hurried and fell into step beside me.

"Not smart enough to figure out why a human was used in this little debacle."

We entered my room and shut the door behind us, almost catching the toes of the goblin that had been following behind. I heard a muffled thud as the creature collided with the shut door and raised an eyebrow at Race.

"What gives with your miniature shadow?" I changed the subject as I went over to the long sofa lining one wall and sunk into it.

"I caught the little guy when he and a few of the others got batted across the room. That entire batch ended up among the casualties and now this one insists that it has a life debt to me."

"That's so sweet," I gushed. "You have a little friend."

Race scowled, but I saw something soften just a bit in his eyes when he glanced at the door. He came over and plopped down beside me, letting out a sigh that sounded as tired as I wanted to feel.

I leaned into him and let my hands run across his expanse of a chest. I glanced up at him, about to perhaps whisper something suggestive when I saw something that made me leap to my feet.

I backed away from him, Sharkmouth coming into play and hands and feet all going switch in a flash.

"Who…what are you?" I spat.

He looked at me with absolute confusion. I saw his hands move to where his weapons normally hung, and the look of realization that he was carrying nothing at all darkened his features. At the same instance, his eyes changed from dark brown to crystal blue.

"I am going to let you try to give me a good reason not to kill you," I said slowly and evenly.

"If you tell me why, then maybe I will at least have a chance." Race stood deliberately and cocked his head to the side.

There was something very real about his tone. Either he was a very good actor…or…okay, I didn't have an 'or' possibility at the moment.

I was torn on what to say and what to keep to myself. I did not want to give him the answers or ability to lie to me. I was in between him and the door and an idea struck me.

I yanked the door open and a goblin tumbled in, landing almost flat on his face. It scrambled up and let out a little yelp of what could have just been surprise, but absolutely sounded like fear.

"You!" I pointed as I yanked the goblin up and threw it onto the couch. "What is your name?"

"Spleen Rupture," the goblin answered, sliding off the couch and onto its feet. It quickly bowed at the waist and remained until I told it to stand up straight.

"Nose Wart," I uttered. Almost faster than a person could blink, my faithful clan leader was before me.

"Yes, Just Ava." He looked around the room, his eyes not even pausing as they passed over Spleen Rupture.

"Is that one of ours?" I pointed to the other goblin.

"Yes, Just Ava."

Well, at least I had that answered. Another idea came. "And is that man over there somebody that you are familiar with?"

Nose Wart looked over at Race and then back to me. His face was twisted into an expression of confusion. "That is the

Templar, Race Mitchell."

"Are you certain?"

Nose Wart squinted at the man and then looked back at me. "Who else would it be?"

"And would you be able to tell if this was an imposter?"

"Imposter?" Race blurted. "What the hell are you talking about, Ava?"

"Your eyes." I decided that I could at least let some of the cat out of the bag.

"My eyes?" He seemed confused, then his face brightened and he started to laugh.

"You may want to share whatever it is that you find amusing," I warned, taking a step towards him. "I am about five seconds away from finding out if whatever you are tastes good."

"Okay." Race held up his hands, his smile gone as it seemed that the gravity of his situation became a bit more real. "I am going to guess that you are referring to my eye color."

"Keep talking."

"When I am in full Templar mode, for lack of a better way to explain it, my eyes are brown. When I let myself relax, or if I am being intimate, then my eyes revert to their natural blue. That color has become enhanced over the centuries for reasons that I do not know. There is a theory that it is a concentration of our former humanity."

I stood there staring for a moment as I tossed all this recent information inwards. Both Betty and Blodwen were quick to confirm and, just that fast, I felt like a total idiot.

"I am so sorry. I have not been able to let my old self come to the surface in so long that I just forgot," Race apologized. "I can't believe it went this long before becoming a thing."

In one long stride, he was to me and had me in his arms. I felt his strong hands slide up my back and then down my sides to plant themselves on my waist. He looked down at me, his blue eyes making me feel like they were sending flames into my core.

"I-I…" My words dried up as I did not actually know what I wanted to say. I wasn't sorry, but by the same token, I'd just about killed and eaten Race Mitchell.

"Shh." He put a finger to my lips and I was happy to discover that Sharkmouth had already retreated on its own. "You don't need to worry about anything when it comes to being careful. I'm glad that you made the discovery and that we were able to put it to rest now versus some time later when we might be involved in more intimate events."

There was a scrabble of feet and I heard the door shut as Nose Wart ushered Spleen Rupture out of the room. The two of us were alone once more.

My hands were now resting on his chest and I could feel his slow, deep breathing. I could hear his heart beating strong and sure. Yet, even now, I could barely get a scent from him other than a male muskiness that had nothing to do with my ability to smell death and every bit to do with my ability to be turned on by him.

"I think I might've just displayed a talent for prophecy," I whispered, the side of my face resting firmly on his muscled physique.

"Excuse me?" Race pulled back just a bit and tipped my chin up with one finger crooked under my chin.

"Well," I smiled devilishly up at him, "I did say that I was about five seconds away from discovering if you tasted good."

***

"Well, this has certainly complicated things," I whispered as I traced abstract swirls on Race's chest.

"It has been complicated for a long time, Ava," Race chuckled. "This simply ups the ante."

"Are we making a mistake?"

Race rolled over on his side to face me. His smile made me warm all over and I had to fight the urge to simply snuggle into his body and forget the entire world.

"I have already thrown my lot in with you. I figure the least we could do is make it enjoyable." A cloud crossed his face, but just as fast, it was gone and his smile broke like the dawn. "I just want you to know that I am here. I'm on your side. There will be some nasty fights ahead, and you don't have to take them all on by yourself. You have Lisa...the goblins will basically throw themselves at anything that threatens you...and I'm here." I opened my mouth and he shushed me with one large index finger. "I know you can handle yourself. I'm not here to rescue or save you, but I am here to back you up. Do you have any idea how hard it was to stay back while you faced off with a demon for crying out loud...and then fight an ogre magi barehanded?"

"So you think I can take care of myself?" I sorta hated sounding like I was seeking his approval; I am a badass, but I guess I really did want to know that Race saw me as an equal and not a damsel-in-distress.

"Absolutely, but like I've been trying to tell you...nobody needs to be an island. Don't think for a moment that I will hesitate a second to call for you if my back is against the wall."

I tried to imagine Race calling on me to help him. I'd seen him knocked across a room while trying to attack a giant. As my mind replayed that particular event, I remembered how I was the one to actually win that fight.

"I've never truly seen a demon," Race admitted. "I have no idea what you came away from that encounter with, but just being in close proximity to that thing caused me to have to fight through an overwhelming desire to just surrender my will."

I popped up and eyed him. I hadn't felt anything of the sort. He had just been another big-mouthed nemesis that I knew would eventually fight me. If it knew what was good for it, that fight would be sooner rather than later. I was only getting stronger. If I actually started to learn how to use some of the abilities that are floating around inside my head, then Vinwoanoch was in serious trouble.

"I didn't really feel anything," I said just as Betty and Blodwen tried to warn me off.

You can't be so trusting, Ava, Betty scolded. *If you make yourself vulnerable to this Templar...you may pause when it comes time to strike.*

With very little effort, I shut every denizen of my mind away someplace secure. Yeah, she might be right; but at this exact moment, I wanted to simply revel in the arms of a man who made me feel amazing in a hundred different ways.

15

Let's Hear it For the Boys

"…and the home…of the…brave," the female sang and I envied her. She had a really good voice, and let's face it, our national anthem is not an easy one to pull off well.

The crowd was in a frenzy all around me as the lights came up on the jam-packed arena. I scanned the area. There had not been an attack or attempt of any sort on Colt since the encounter in the warehouse. My theory that this had all been a ruse to try and get me out in the open was looking pretty good.

"Here." Race nudged me and handed me one of the dark blue towels that had been handed out at the door. I took it and raised it above my head, twirling it with reckless abandon like pretty much everybody else.

The team from Philadelphia was gathered to my right in a huge circle. Each player had his arms over the shoulders of the man to his left and right. They swayed back and forth while the man in the open center of the ring barked out a variety of things that received a response from the men around him.

I stood up on my tippy toes in order to find both Colt and Anthony. Both men were acting like nothing at all out of the ordinary had occurred these past couple of weeks. I did notice that Colt was making it a point of not looking my way as he finished warming up.

The coin toss put our defense on the field first and I watched Anthony closely for the first couple of plays. He'd insisted that nothing had been done to him during his time as hostage. I just found it a little hard to believe that they hadn't roughed him up even a little bit.

On the first play for Philadelphia, Anthony made a case for being perfectly fine as he shrugged a pair of offensive linemen aside and then engulfed the quarterback for his first sack of the game.

The crowd went wild, and I was right there with them. When we took over possession of the ball I focused on Colt with everything I had. The first play rocketed into motion with his barking cadence. A pair of defensive linemen blew through our offensive line and had the quarterback in their sights.

"Duck!" I screamed as one of the huge men launched himself through the air.

Of course, my voice was only one of thousands yelling the same thing or something very similar. Despite that, I could've sworn that he flinched and did exactly as I'd said just in time for the first defensive player to zoom past overhead. The second defensive player came low a split second later. Colt leapt and hurled the ball at the last possible moment.

It flew like a missile into the outstretched hands of Treyvon Webb who did a front flip into the end zone and then leapt up into the arms of the fans crowded against the padded walls that circled the entire playing area. Just that fast, we were on the board and in the lead.

I tried not to be swept up into the excitement, but it was infectious as our lead increased only to have Philadelphia roar back in the second quarter. The game went to halftime with us clinging to a slim one point lead due to—who else—Anthony Riddle blocking an extra point attempt with one huge paw.

I stood like pretty much everybody else in the place and headed up the stairs. Unlike the vast majority of spectators headed for the concessions or the restrooms, I made the familiar trek back to the locker room entrances.

I took a spot against a wall and did my best to blend in. Unlike previous times, I'd gone through the trouble of being air-brushed so that I basically fit in with the humans. As I stood in an out of the way corner, I enjoyed the smells and interesting conversations of people who walked past with the belief that they were anonymous.

"…that one cheerleader should perhaps accept that she is a size larger than her uniform. I swear she is going to bust out of those shorts if she bends over too fast…"

"…what do you mean we never do what you like? I went to the mall with you last week…"

"…but you missed him twice. Give me the damn dart gun. He will crumple and the team with him."

Wait…what?

I dialed in my hearing and tried to locate the source of that conversation. The first thing that came as I narrowed my search was a very familiar and unpleasant smell.

Vampires? I thought.

While it is true that I eat the dead, vampires are not on my menu. They smell like chocolate caked frosted with Dumpster drippings. I don't know why…that's just the way it is.

My nose brought me through the long service corridor that ran under the arena by the locker rooms. There were no humans near and I quickly spotted the pair of vampires. I tapped into the focus I'd picked up when I'd bonded with Morgan and felt their wrongness.

Take one of them alive, I heard Morgan whisper from wherever she happened to be at the moment.

I could also sense her annoyance at the fact that still more Supernaturals were in her territory without her having sensed them until just this moment. I'd told her all about the demon, but she'd sort of been like the Morgan of old in that she did not clue me in on whatever it was that she might be gleaning from what I'd shared.

The biggest problem that I was having at the moment, though, was in the fact that apparently Colt was still a target. If simply drawing me out had been the purpose of going after him in the first place, then by all rights he should be safe now. So why wasn't he? Also, why kill the guy? I mean, wouldn't it be a lot easier to just kidnap him for a while and then let him go after the football game?

Oh well. I guess I was back on the clock.

"You guys wouldn't be trying to ruin my team's chances of winning the championship?" I said, breaking the relative silence.

It isn't often that you get to startle a vampire. By the reactions of these two, it was clear I'd done exactly that as they both whirled about. One of them dropped something that looked like a very expensive dart gun. Both of them had fangs bared and eyes burning red. That last part was new. I would have to ask Belinda about that later. I don't believe that I'd ever seen her with glowing red eyes before.

"Ava Birch," one of the vampires said. The thing is, he wasn't saying it to me; it sounded more like he was reporting it or perhaps sharing it with his colleague.

"You realize that this is not gonna go well for either of you," I said calmly. "And here is the deal...I only need one of you. So one of you is going to be nothing more than vampire dust when this encounter is over. The other will be coming along with me as a prisoner for the most part. Do I have any volunteers?"

The two vamps looked at each other, then at me, and then back at each other. Then they started laughing.

"Is that right?" I snapped.

I bounded for them and was not surprised when they both moved in opposite directions. I now had one of them on each side, which was exactly what I had been hoping for. My next move was for the one on my right. I'd been planning that jump already and was very happy to see my plan actually working out the way I intended.

You really should know better, a voice that I actually think was my own scolded.

I brought a hand across with the intention of decapitating this vampire. Honestly, it really didn't make a difference which one of them I captured and which one I killed. The sparks that flew off my switch-fingers from where I made contact with the series of pipes that ran along the corridor were only secondary to the searing pain that jolted my entire being and sent me flying back about ten or twenty feet in the direction of the other vampire who was waiting for me. This one punched me and sent me back like a tennis ball towards the one that I'd struck.

A vampire is strong. I'd just discovered exactly how strong as my ribs on the left side felt like they exploded into splinters. It was the equivalent of being hit by a sledgehammer swung by a circus strongman.

I was getting to my hands and knees when a booted foot connected with my other side and shattered more ribs. This time I landed on my back. For some reason, the song *99 Luft Balloons* started in my head. Thank goodness, because that last shot was really painful.

I made it to my feet as both vampires came at me in a blur from both sides. My brain managed to slow things down somehow. In that instant, I had a strange sense of clarity. I wondered if this was how Colt felt when he had those two defensive linemen coming for him earlier. In any case, that was what I used as my inspiration as I ducked, letting the first one fly over my head, missing me completely. The second one also missed as I took a step forward and plastered myself against the wall of the long corridor.

"Don't make this any more difficult on yourself than you need to," one of the vampires crooned as they each crouched in preparation for the next attack.

I'd been lucky once—twice actually since I'd dodged a pair of attacks—but I did not think both of them would miss a second time. I braced myself for whatever was coming and made a mental note that I would take out the vampire on my right. It was completely arbitrary, but if I was going to go down, then I was taking one of them with me.

"What do we have here?" a voice said from the entrance to the tunnel that I'd used. I shot a glance that way, but the voice's owner was obviously smart enough not to step out and be visible.

"Kayleeni?" I gulped. "What are you doing here?"

"I could ask you the same question, Ava," the water elf replied, still remaining out of sight.

"You know me...just nosing around. I found these two vampires who are obviously in Morgan's district without permission. I guess they still want to kill Colt for whatever reason. So much for the theory that the attempts on his life were just to flush me out."

"You still haven't figured out why?" Kayleeni chuckled. "I guess he is still human, so why would you." That last bit was a statement, not a question.

"Care to fill me in?" I called. I was getting a really bad feeling in the pit of my stomach. I'd been duped by a mud troll that had me believing she was an innocent victim. Had this water elf done the same thing?

"How about we just kill you and get this over with?" one of the vampires snapped. I made the choice that I was going to kill the one to my left now since he was sporting such an attitude.

"Oh...there will be killing," another familiar voice hissed with a tinge of anger.

"Race!" I gasped. I didn't want to sound like I needed saving, but at the moment, being saved was not something I would complain too loudly about.

"Can't leave you alone for a moment, can I, babe?"

He called me 'babe'? We would talk about that later. I am cool with the opening of doors, but I wasn't much for the cutesy nickname stuff.

"So, what brings you down here?" I asked, trying to sound casual.

"Excuse me!" one of the vampires barked. "Can we get back to the business at hand. Although it does seem that we will be adding to the menu." This vamp made an over-dramatic point of sniffing the air. "I don't believe that I have feasted on Templar in ages. This is a treat."

"And what am I...chopped liver?" Kayleeni actually sounded hurt. "Or do you have water elves as a regular part of your diet?"

"Are we seriously arguing over who the vampires get to

148

eat?" I grumbled.

"Oh…we wouldn't eat you," the most vocal of the pair scoffed. "Ghouls are disgusting creatures whose blood has gone rancid."

Yeah…I was definitely going to kill the one on the left.

As if they had some sort of telepathic link, the two vampires launched once more. I was really happy to see the one on the left flying at me while the one on the right made for Race.

I actually stepped into the vamp as it slammed into me. Sure, the pain flared bright, but hearing Madonna sing about being a *Material Girl* was enough to force it down to nothing more than a dull throb in the back of my consciousness.

My claws plunged into its body. That was not enough to kill, but I was pleased to see that vampires still feel pain to some degree. This one howled as I yanked my hands back, but that sound ended the moment I made a swipe that severed its head.

There was a sizzling sound and then my vampire exploded in a cloud of sparkling grit. Just as mine evaporated in a swirl of coarse glitter, I heard the roar of the crowd that indicated the teams were taking the field for the second half of play.

"Ava!" Race bellowed. Out of instinct, I ducked.

The second vampire hissed at me as it flew past. "Your days are numbered, ghoul!"

A strange popping noise sounded and the angry blood sucker was gone. Looking around, I saw Race slumped against the wall. Kayleeni was kneeling beside him. I rushed to his side, afraid of what I might find.

"I hate vampires," the Templar growled.

I saw a nasty rip down his right shoulder. Even with all the blood, I was barely getting a whiff of anything from him. I was about to ask if there was anything I could do when the ring on his finger, the special one all Templars wear, began to glow a soft blue. I swear I could see the flesh mending as I watched.

"I gotta hang out with you guys more often," Kayleeni said as she leaned so close to Race's injury that I thought her nose was going to actually touch the knitting wound.

A moment later, it was as if nothing had happened…except

for the blood all over his clothes. As he stood up, I realized that we hadn't managed to snag one of the vampires as Morgan asked. Since I was not sure how this new link between the two of us worked, I tried to focus on Morgan, then I sent a mental version of a report telling what all happened.

I didn't actually get an answer, but I felt something that made me believe that my accounts of our little scrap were received. I could tell this was going to have a steep learning curve. And I'd just felt like I was making ground in things.

Lifting my shirt, I expected to see bones jutting out from the skin. Instead, I was just a mottled darker gray in spots.

"Do you need to eat?" Kayleeni asked, moving over now to inspect me with the same degree of uncomfortable closeness that she'd shown inspecting Race.

"Not right this moment," I said after I did a bit of self-inventory. I was sore, but I did not feel like I would lose my mind and sink into the *Fame Rabia*. Maybe I'd only thought my ribs splintered

"Hey, Kayleeni," Race turned to the water elf. "Can you dash up to the concessions area and grab me a tee-shirt or jersey?"

She accepted a handful of bills and departed, mumbling something about not being anybody's servant. Together, Race and I made our way to the entrance of the tunnel that led to the field. We jockeyed for position until we could see the huge monitor suspended above the playing area.

As we watched the game and waited for blood-free clothing for him to arrive that he could wear back to our seats, we reflected on how nice it was to be with somebody that did not feel the need to rehash what we'd just been through. Also, he made no attempt to get me to make silly promises about never doing anything like that again. The fact was that he'd come to watch my back just as he promised.

"Until that second one nailed you, I assumed you had the situation under control."

I really wanted to kiss him for that remark. Of course it didn't hurt that he was standing there stripped to the waist. At last, Kayleeni showed up. Race donned the shirt, not making a comment that it was bright pink and obviously meant for a woman with its snug fit at the waist.

We made it back to our seats just as the third quarter was coming to an end. The clock was ticking down the final seconds as Colt hurled another missile deep downfield. Treyvon Webb went horizontal as he dove to make yet another spectacular catch.

My eyes had been so fixed on the wide receiver and his amazing catch that I completely missed the two defenders sandwiching Colt. There was a collective groan and gasp from the crowd and I jerked around to see the still form sprawled on the turf.

A hush fell over the crowd as several players and a trio that I had to assume to be doctors or medical staff of some sort all hurried out to the motionless body. I locked my senses onto the pair who had made the hit. Neither gave me anything other than a regular human smell of eventual death. Unfortunately, that scent was being drowned by another more familiar smell that seeped into every bit of my being.

It was as if that smell reminded me that my ribs were pretty banged up. I felt a throbbing in my chest that vibrated every single rib; or at least that is the way it felt.

"He's dead," I whispered to Race.

As we watched an ambulance roll out onto the field, I could hear the murmurs of people speculating. I wanted to yell what I knew to be a fact, but that seemed grossly inappropriate. I have no idea how long I'd been standing there watching this terrible event unspool when something tugged on my arm.

"We need to go," Kayleeni urged.

"What?" I yanked my arm free and scowled at the water elf. Why would we go anywhere? A man was dead out on that field. I'd failed.

"You need to be there when he wakes up."

That sentence hung in the air for several seconds before I shook my head and asked, "What are you talking about?"

"He will change. You need to snag his body and get him

someplace safe so that he isn't gutted and stuffed in a box or cremated."

"I still don't know what you are talking about."

"Colt is going to turn," Kayleeni insisted.

"Into what?" Why wasn't this clicking? And why did I feel like I was missing the obvious.

"A ghoul."

16

Urgent

"I still don't see how you could know such a thing," I grumbled as I shut the door and started down the stairs to the lower level of my house.

"It has been years of researching bloodlines," Kayleeni said. I could tell she was tired of repeating herself. "I would have been here for you if you hadn't changed your name."

"I didn't change it...I just adjusted it a bit," I replied defensively.

I'd actually seen the book the water elf kept with the history of a dozen bloodlines that she'd managed to trace to the current era. The most disturbing fact from all of what I'd seen was the winding path my genetic line took all the way back to a single name: Boudicca.

As I stepped into one of the larger rooms, I was greeted by Morgan and two women that I did not recognize. I could sense something almost leaking from the pair that reminded me of fresh cut grass.

"Witches?" I asked as I joined the Psychic.

"Yes, and I hope you don't mind, but I would like for them to remain here in your house," Morgan said with a nod.

"How come you didn't show up to my house with witches?" I refrained from committing to her request. Sure, I was probably going to say yes, but I was annoyed about the degree of attention that this transformation Colt would be making was getting from everybody.

"You did not demonstrate prior to your transformation," Morgan replied matter-of-factly.

I would let her slide for now, but that didn't mean I liked it. Looking around, I was surprised to see Rain and the faeries present as well as three men off to the side with Race that I had to assume were also Templars based on their Men-in-Black apparel.

"Did you know?" I asked.

"Not even a little. I still can't believe that this is the gentleman you had in your house and that you were hired to protect." Morgan pushed away from the wall and came around to face me. When she spoke, her lips barely moved and I knew that this was intended for just me. "I now believe that whoever was trying to have this young man assassinated was aware of his lineage. If it was the demon, then we have a new problem."

I waited for a moment to see if she would tell me. As we stood in silence, a question bloomed in my head. It took all I had not to blurt it. I tried her trick of just moving my lips. I sure wish our limited telepathic communication ability worked inside my home.

"I thought that a person had to commit suicide to become a ghoul." I shot that same thought in to Betty and Blodwen. Surprisingly, I received no response from the pair.

"Males differ slightly in that respect. Of course, until Mr. Faber, we always believed that this transformation only took place with soldiers who died in combat. Apparently, whatever mystical force is responsible for the conversion was activated because Colt was engaged in an adversarial endeavor."

"Okay...now can you explain that in common words?" I grumped.

"A male ghoul turns if he loses his life in a situation where he is pitted against an enemy...even if it is figurative."

We stood in silence as we simply waited for the change to happen. As we did, I considered the situation that I now faced. It was clear that the war was indeed upon us. I now held more be-ings in my mind that were hostile towards me than I did those that were willing to help.

It just wasn't fair. In all the stupid books I have read or the movies that I've watched...the end of the story has a satisfying victory for the hero or heroine. Mine were only getting worse. And now I had some demon pissed at me and set on my destruc-tion.

I had failed in my task at keeping Colt alive. His death, while not technically my fault, and not committed by a Super-natural, had still yielded the same results. We were all sitting around waiting for him to open his eyes and join our community.

"Whoever wanted him dead probably intended to take his body," Morgan said, jerking me back to our conversation.

Well, I guess I could claim a win there. It had been very lit-tle trouble to lie in wait for the ambulance as it drove to the hospital. They weren't in any hurry since there was no danger that their patient would slip into an even worse condition. Race had taken out the driver and the man riding in back with Colt's body at the first stop light. It had been a simple matter of hop-ping out of my car and rushing up to the driver's side window.

"Help!" he'd gasped, slapping the window. As soon as the driver had opened the door, probably out of instinct, Race had yanked him out and put him asleep quickly and painlessly. The guy in back had opened those back doors and been blasted by a small wand that Kayleeni was carrying. It had basically para-lyzed him. I sorta felt sorry for the guy. His eyes were darting back and forth as we carried him to the side of the road and laid him beside his friend.

We weren't any closer to dealing with the undead obliterat-ing death ray gun. And shortly after I arrived home, Morgan had reported to me that Portland had been ex-communicated as a ter-ritory by the Psychic Council. When I asked what that meant, her answer was very blunt, and I was suddenly longing for the days when she didn't tell me anything.

"Every Supernatural in this district is considered null. There will be a concentrated effort to eliminate every single one that remains after the forty-eight-hour grace period expires."

I looked around the room with all the goblins, bugbears, fairies, and even a few creatures that I've never seen before. I was hit by a realization.

"They are here for protection?"

"No," Morgan said with a laugh. "They are here to pledge their support. They are declaring their intention to remain. This is the beginnings of our army."

"And so it is this roomful against the world?" I asked, not very enthused about our chances.

"No. Most of the Supernatural world will sit out this battle. It will be up to the Psychics who have fallen in with the Council to send in their invaders. Many of them will even be pitting against each other."

"That makes no sense." I gave a dismissive wave. "If they want you...*us*...if they want us gone so badly, then why not team up and just overwhelm us with numbers?"

"That might've been an option until recently. You have to understand that you are the prize that is going to be fought over."

"Wait...what?" I shouted, spinning on Morgan. Every set of eyes in the room had turned in my direction, but I didn't care. "I'm no damn prize."

"I think I would agree with you," Race said with a smile curling his lips up as he moved to take a spot beside me.

"Shut up, you." I gave him a sharp elbow in the ribs.

"There are two ghouls in my district," Morgan said. "That is unheard of. Whether we are ready or not...whether we like it or not...war is here, and you are at the center of it, Ava."

I briefly wondered if it was too late to go back and reclaim that territory in Dallas.

"He is waking!" a voice called from the room where Colt had been stored.

Oh well, looks like I'm stuck here. And in case you were wondering...we lost that stupid indoor football championship game when the backup quarterback threw an interception that was returned for a touchdown in the final minute. I wonder if Colt will believe me when I tell him that I need to slap him once just to get his powers jumpstarted?

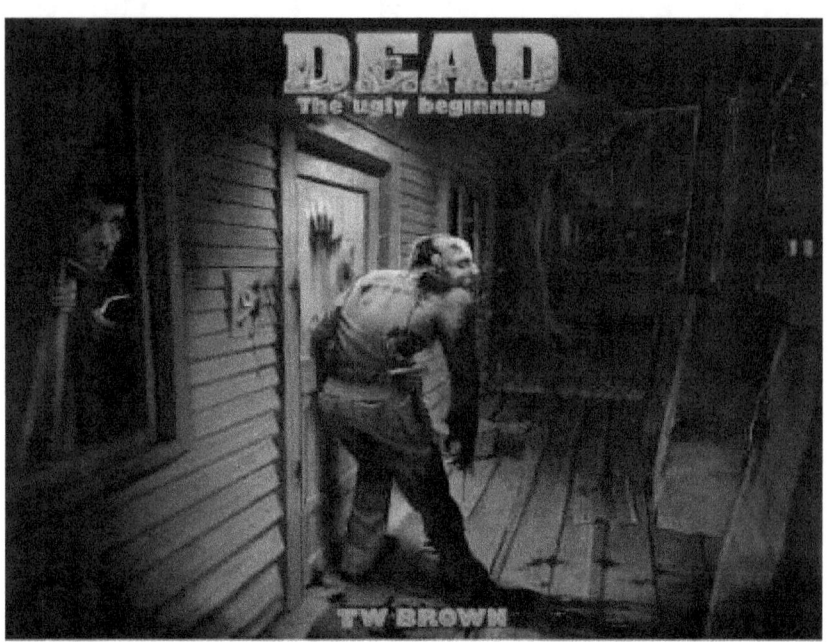

Step into the DEAD world created by TW Brown -
Follow along with the DEAD - the 12 book series starting with
The Ugly Beginning - or enjoy a few laughs following Ava
Birch's adventures in the horror/comedy That Ghoul Ava

MAY DECEMBER
Publications

**The growing voice in horror
and speculative fiction.**

Find us at www.maydecemberpublications.com
Or
Email us at contact@maydecemberpublications.com

TW Brown is the author of the ***Zomblog*** series, his horror comedy romp, ***That Ghoul Ava***, and, of course, the ***DEAD*** series. Safely tucked away in the beautiful Pacific Northwest, he moves away from his desk only at the urging of his Border Collie, Aoife. (Pronounced Eye-fa)

He plays a little guitar on the side...just for fun...and makes up any excuse to either go trail hiking or strolling along his favorite place...Cannon Beach. He answers all his emails sent to twbrown.maydecpub @gmail.com and tries to thank everybody personally when they take the time to leave a review of one of his works.

His blog can be found at:http://twbrown.blogspot.com

The best way to find everything he has out is to start at his Author Page:

You can follow him on twitter @maydecpub and on Facebook under Todd Brown, Author TW Brown, and also under May December Publications.

www.ingramcontent.com/pod-product-compliance
Lightning Source LLC
Chambersburg PA
CBHW071251130626
46556CB00003B/1261